COURT OF DARKNESS

INSTITUTE OF THE SHADOW FAE: BOOK TWO

C.N. CRAWFORD

❀ Created with Vellum

CHAPTER 1

I had less than a minute before the dragon shifter found me in his bedroom. The rich bastard had a private lift that opened right into his hallway. Through his bedroom doorway, I could see the numbers ticking up as the lift rose from the lobby. *Two...three...*

If it reached forty-one, the jig was up.

Frantically, I scanned the room. I stood on the forty-first floor of a sleek skyscraper in the center of London. Wind whipped into the room from the open balcony door. Moonlight streamed in through the expansive windows, casting silvery light over tasteful gray and gold furniture. From here, the gleaming lights of London spread out below like glittering treasure.

Only problem was, I couldn't find the actual treasure, and that was the whole reason I'd come.

The lift's number ticked up. *Eight...nine...*

The white spotlight from my headlamp bounced all over the darkened room. Where the hells was he keeping his gold? All dragon shifters had gold. This one wasn't big on clutter, so it hadn't taken long to ransack his entire flat. Hunger gripped my stomach. Ciara and I were starving, and I was *not* leaving empty-handed. The great heroine Ciarianna would rise again.

My stomach rumbled. In the past week, we'd had nothing to eat but three tins of economy beans and two ice cream sandwiches. I could hardly think straight. I hadn't felt this hungry since I'd murdered the Institute's hunger fae.

Twelve...thirteen...

The bathroom. I hadn't fully investigated the bathroom yet, and he had a medicine cabinet I needed to rifle through. I rushed into the bathroom, flinging open the cabinet.

I blinked. Among the painkillers and some anti-anxiety medication, the shifter had filled his cabinet with Barbie dolls and plastic dinosaur figurines. Not to mention two tubs of Vaseline.

What in the world…?

I didn't dwell on it too long, because in the next second, I was crouching down to search under the sink. Toilet roll, cleaning products, an enormous vat of Vaseline. I mean, I supposed a dragon shifter's scales *would* get dry in the winter.

Twenty...twenty-one...

Under his bed. I hadn't yet searched under his bed. It was a stupid place to hide gold, but I hadn't found a sensible hiding place. Like a safe.

I knelt down and flung up the silver duvet. The white light from my headlamp beamed over a bunch of magazines.

I pulled one out, and my jaw dropped. First of all, in this day and age, who read porn in magazine form? And more importantly—where did one find magazines featuring women mating with men dressed as dinosaurs?

I mean, I supposed when you thought about it, maybe it made a strange sort of sense. Dragon-on-human porn would get old after a while, and he'd need to up the ante. One kink level up from dragons was obviously dinosaurs, and—

Twenty-nine...thirty...

Right. The gold. My wild hunger was making me get sidetracked. Still, I was taking one of these magazines with me because no one would ever believe—

On second thought, maybe I didn't really want to touch it. Thinking of all the Vaseline, I dropped it with a grimace.

Thirty-four...thirty-five...

I leapt up, scanning the room again. Now, adrenaline raced through my veins. I was out of time. I touched the lumen stone around my neck—on loan from the Wraith—and reassured myself that I still had a way out of here. Shadow-leaping came in *very* handy sometimes, even at six hundred feet in the air.

Then, my gaze landed on the one thing in the flat I hadn't yet searched. A potted orchid that stood on a mahogany table in his bedroom. A perfect hiding place.

Thirty-eight...thirty-nine...

I thrust my hand into the soil, and relief washed over me as my fingers came into contact with a smooth, metallic bar.

Bingo.

Forty-one.

The lift doors slid open just as I ripped the gold bar from the plant. Dirt flew all over the shifter's sleek gray sofa. I slid my bug-out bag off my shoulder and shoved the bar into it.

Now, I just needed to find a way out. Good thing I'd been practicing shadow-leaping. I touched the lumen stone, summoning its icy power as I rushed out onto the balcony.

Behind me, the dragon shifter roared, already transforming into his reptilian form. Scales were forming on his face and arms, but if he fully shifted in here, he'd break everything in the bloody flat. He was practically vibrating with the effort to restrain himself. Talons began to sprout from his fingertips.

I scrambled over the wooden table on his balcony, then

climbed onto the short barrier of glass. Adrenaline raced through my veins as the view dizzied me. The lights of Spitalfields twinkled below me. Gods, this was high.

The shifter screamed something, but since he kept shifting and pulling back to his human form, it came out all garbled. Half-dragon speak. Something like *mablig blupart plucking skrill you!*

I stood on the glass barrier, the wind tearing at my hair, and my heart raced out of control. *Time to go.*

A blast of hot fire seared the air behind me, and I leapt off the balcony before I had a chance to properly choose my target.

I gripped hard to my backpack straps as I started falling, the wind whipping my hair into my face. My stomach lurched, and I started to regret several of the night's decisions.

Through the strands of my lavender hair, I spotted a dark corner of Wormwood Street. Mentally, I melded with its shadows, smelling the seared-air scent of the magic within all darkness. Then, I channeled my shadow magic. I leapt.

I slammed hard onto concrete, rolling over the ground with a grunt. Pretty sure the gold bar in my backpack left a dent in my spine.

The impact had rattled my bones. So, I was learning that shadow leaping when you're already falling at a high velocity only took *some* of the impact out of the fall. If I were human, I'd be dead now. But as a demi-fae, I escaped with a few fractures and a shitload of bruises.

My gaze flicked up the sleek skyscraper. Dragons could fly, but there was no way this guy was coming after me. Supernaturals had been completely outlawed for the past four years. Executions and assassinations meant the shifters had to lay low, disguise themselves completely. Which meant I could take his gold bar—

My thoughts were interrupted by the sight of a man's silhouette plunging off the balcony, just as I'd done. My pulse began to race. This wasn't what I'd expected.

The dragon shifter started to fall, his descent picking up pace, until—midair—black, scaly wings burst from his back.

Okay. Maybe I'd overestimated his intelligence. With a flagrant display of magic like this, he'd be dead within a day, never to defile his dinosaur figurines again.

In the air, he shifted completely, rearing back his head to eject a hot stream of fire into the midnight sky.

Oh boy. London hadn't seen a reptilian display like this in years.

I jumped up, eyeing the farthest point I could see on Wormwood Street. At this time of night, the streets were mercifully empty.

I summoned the icy shadow magic, channeling it throughout my limbs. Then, I melded with the dark pools of shadows under a pedestrian crossway. I began shadow-leaping through the financial district—past pharmacies and skyscrapers—using alleyways and the darkness beneath the trees lining the street. The wind rushed over my skin, and my heart hammered from the flight. I leapt into a medieval churchyard, melding with the shadows behind a crooked tomb. It was three in the morning, and I hardly passed anyone.

But while I raced through the city, moving like the wind through the trees, the dragon soared just above me, managing to track my path. His fire scalded the air. I glanced up, my blood roaring, as he started to dive for me.

With the magic igniting my body, I shadow-leapt across the street. I needed to hide from him, to go underground. Fortunately, I used to live under the streets, and I knew how to navigate subterranean London.

I leapt south, zooming closer to Guildhall, until I

screeched to a halt by a manhole. Beneath this pavement flowed one of London's underground rivers.

A wild roar ripped through the skies as I glanced up, my heart skipping a beat, and saw the dragon dive-bombing for me.

With a grunt, I shifted the manhole cover. I jumped into the hole and dropped down into three feet of freezing, stinking water. From above, a blast of fire exploded through the manhole opening, singeing the hair on the back of my arms. With magic flowing through my body, I leapt away into the tunnel's darkness.

Underground, shadows reigned. Only the bouncing white light of my headlamp pierced the darkness.

The dragon's enormous body wouldn't be able to fit through the hole, and in his human form, he'd never catch up with me. Now, the tunnel was mine. I leapt through the darkness, the water growing higher and higher on my body, past my hips, my ribs, until it covered my head.

I dove deeper into the cold water, swimming under the surface. Once underwater, I wasn't able to shadow-leap, and my lungs started to burn. My headlamp flickered out.

At this point, the dragon must be long gone. I could only hope he hadn't been clever enough to predict where I'd emerge out of the tunnel.

Just when I was certain my lungs were about to explode, thin streams of light pierced the water as the tunnel opened up into the Thames—London's largest river, no longer underground.

I kicked my feet as hard as I could, rushing up to the surface. I gasped, sucking in air. I scrambled for the stone embankment, then hoisted myself over the edge. A quick glance at the sky told me that the dragon hadn't caught up with me yet.

Unfortunately, a low iron fence blocked my path to the

pavement. Iron would burn me if I touched it, though it wouldn't kill me.

Grimacing, I gripped the iron bars, wincing at the pain. Fast as I could, I climbed it, then leapt over the top. Exhausted, I flung myself down on the pavement. I rolled over on my back, my backpack bulky beneath my spine. I stared up at the night sky, catching my breath.

It took me a moment to get my bearings. I'd ended up just south of the river. Here, the streetlamps cast amber light over an empty walkway and neat rows of plane trees. My little white sundress clung to my body.

It wasn't just the underwater swim that had exhausted me, but the overuse of shadow magic. My muscles buzzed and burned. Shadow magic wasn't native to my body like it was to Ruadan's. I could draw it from the lumen stone, but it tended to overwhelm me and wear me out. This must be what drug addicts felt like on a comedown.

On the pavement, I closed my eyes for just a moment, still gasping for air, when a familiar power brushed over my skin —a dark, sensual magic that raised goosebumps on my body.

When I opened my eyes, I was staring into the penetrating, violet gaze of Ruadan.

CHAPTER 2

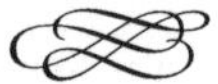

Moonlight sculpted the perfect planes of his face. My heart thumped harder against my ribs.

I clasped my hand to my chest, staring up at him.

When I'd imagined running into Ruadan again, I hadn't pictured myself lying flat on my back in a dress soaked in dirty river water.

"Hi, Ruadan." The sight of him sent a rush of energy through my blood, but I feigned a casual tone. "What are you doing here skulking by the riverside?"

A gust of wind picked up his cloak. I glimpsed the armor that gleamed underneath, sculpting his body. His shadowy magic lashed the air around him, and a shiver rippled over my wet skin.

My stomach loudly rumbled, giving away my hunger. "You can calm down with your menacing display of magic." I pushed myself up, sitting upright. "You're already dressed like a medieval undertaker. The shadows are just intimidation overkill."

The wind rustled through the nearby leaves.

"Back to your silence, then. Even though you killed Baleros and completed your task." I pushed a lock of sodden lavender hair out of my eyes. "Did you know that dinosaur porn exists?"

So quiet it was almost inaudible, I heard a low growl rumble from Ruadan's chest, and the sound trembled through my gut.

The silence stretched on. Then, as I looked up at Ruadan, a wild roar rent the air. My body tensed, as a burst of flame cut across the sky. The dragon had found me, and he was dive-bombing again, unleashing his fire.

Ruadan unsheathed the sword on his back, whirling to face the dragon. An intense pulse of icy magic burst through the air, and violet magic danced over his sword.

As the dragon raced for us—only twenty feet away now—shadow-magic exploded from Ruadan's sword. It slammed into the dragon's chest, and ice frosted the creature's scales. Instantly, the dragon's flames were snuffed out. As it screeched to a stop on the pavement, Ruadan leapt. He swung his blade, and it carved into the dragon's neck. Blood arced into the air.

The dragon's head rolled onto the pavement, his dark eyes wide. The creature's body shuddered, then slumped to the ground with a loud *thud*. The two detached pieces—head and body—shifted back into their human form one final time.

When Ruadan turned back to me, cold fury had darkened his eyes. I couldn't say he looked particularly happy to see me.

I stood, my teeth chattering. I crossed my arms, wishing I'd worn something other than white for my little river swim. My dress looked completely transparent, and I felt vulnerable enough standing in front of Ruadan.

Ruadan crossed to a plane tree, just behind the dragon

shifter's headless corpse. To my surprise, he knelt before the tree. He lifted his sword, and plunged it into the soil that surrounded the tree's base. He bowed his head, as if in prayer. His body glowed with violet light, and I breathed in his scent—apples and pine. It was a strangely seductive smell, one that curled around my shivering body, warming me from the inside out.

It took me a moment to figure out what he was doing, until I cast my mind back to Grand Master Savus's little history lesson. The Shadow Fae didn't think of themselves as assassins. They viewed themselves as servants of the old fae gods—gods who demanded sacrifices. In Ruadan's mind, the dragon's death had been a sacrifice—blood to feed the soil of those older than even the fae.

When he rose, the coldness in his eyes sent a shiver up my spine. They had gone completely dark.

Shadows in an incubus's eyes meant one of two things: he was turned on, or he wanted to kill someone. And unless I was way off about Ruadan's tastes, I didn't imagine that dragon decapitation got him in the mood.

I cleared my throat. "You said you'd find me, and now you have. Well done. Your tracking abilities are without parallel."

His silence never failed to unnerve me, and his low growl slid through my bones. As his eyes pierced me, a gust of wind toyed with his hair. His tightly coiled body language was that of an animal about to attack its prey.

I heaved a sigh. "How I've missed your sparkling personality." I touched the lumen stone at my neck. "I thought you could speak again, now that you killed Baleros."

Blood-chilling stillness from the Wraith. I was starting to get the impression he was annoyed that I'd been using the lumen stone to burgle gold.

"Look, I'm staying with my human friend, Ciara," I said. "She and I needed to eat. You said you'd be back for me, and that I wasn't finished at the Institute. But I had no idea when that would be. We spent a month in Scotland, unemployed and starving. I managed to find a bar job for one week, but my boss thought he could withhold my paycheck until I showed him my boobs. Naturally, I was forced to throw him through a window, after which point my employment was unceremoniously terminated. Which was absurd, frankly. Humans are so sensitive about scrapes and bruises."

The only sound around us was the rushing of the river behind me. The lethal look in Ruadan's eyes promised violence. Somehow, that was my cue to continue.

"So, we came back to London," I went on. "I mean, it's not like we could hide from the Shadow Fae, anyway. You know how to find me. Rufus wouldn't hire us back. Do you know where we've been living?" I took a step closer, working up a bit of a temper. "In one of those burnt-out cars under the arches by that goat pen. That's right. Just off the park where Uncle Darrell makes sweet, sweet love to the earth—a sight that has greeted me every morning for the past three weeks. That image will be forever burned into my mind, the dawn light ruddying his arse cheeks as he thrusts gamely into the soil. I blame you for this memory."

I took another step closer, now jabbing him in the chest, which felt like poking a brick wall. "Before you wafted into my life in a puff of smoke, I had a job. I had a flat." I cocked my head. "I know. I know. I didn't have a fancy rock bed or black stones glittering in my walls like you have, but I had crisp packets on my floor. They were *my* crisp packets. My flat. My life. Now, I'm out of a job, out of a place to live. I've got no money. Do you know what I had for breakfast this morning? A half-eaten Egg McMuffin that a janitor threw out at Liverpool Street station. I'm *starving,* and so is Ciara."

I lifted the lumen stone. "But at least you left me with this. So what's the best way to get a shitload of money in one go?

Shadow-leaping into a dragon-shifter's flat. One bar of gold, and Ciara and I are set for decades. You can hardly fault me for that. It was perfectly reasonable."

Ruadan loomed over me. His magic seemed to suck in the light from all around us, and flecks of starlight glinted in his eyes. It was hard to forget that he was a demigod—a god of the night.

He held out a black-gloved hand.

"Of course you want the gold. Because it's not enough to take my job, my flat, and my vaguely functioning life. You also have to take the gold bar that's rightfully mine by virtue of burglary."

"It belongs to the Institute."

"Interesting. So you can speak."

He held out his hand to me. "The gold."

"Fine." I jammed my hand into my sodden backpack. I'd find another, more subtle way to steal if I had to. "The Institute are a bunch of thieves, you know that?" Perhaps this wasn't the best night to go around accusing others of thievery, but irritation was simmering and I hadn't thought of a better insult. "You're the Mafia, just with swords and a pretense of sacrifice."

"I don't think you've fully absorbed the seriousness of your situation."

I blinked, still irritated. "No, I haven't absorbed anything whatsoever. Do you know why? Because you just stand there staring at me with your magic whipping all over the place and no words coming out of your mouth." I jabbed him in the torso again, my finger crooking at the steel in his chest. "If you want me to *absorb* things, you can tell them to me in words. I will accept writing on paper. Am I on the kill list now, or am I coming back to the Institute?"

He pivoted, already stalking off into the shadows. "You're coming with me."

Of course, that wasn't as many details as I'd hoped for, and I couldn't say the timing was ideal.

"Now?" I hurried after him, gripping the straps of my backpack. I pulled off my headlamp, which had broken underwater. "Where are we going?"

"The Institute. You're returning."

"I live with my friend Ciara now." I was giving too much away here. I was letting Ruadan know exactly how to get to me—the same way Baleros had. "I look after Ciara. She's waiting for me to come home with some kind of food. If she stays on her own, she's vulnerable. Honestly, we were just getting our lives back together."

A sweep of his eyes up and down my body gave me a hint of what he was thinking. Something along the lines of, *What do you mean you are getting your life together? You look like a drowned Victorian prostitute and you live in a burnt car.*

Or, I may have been projecting my own internal thoughts onto him. Hard to say.

He pivoted. "Let's not forget the reality of your situation. You stole from the Institute. You stabbed me—"

"I *did* apologize. In written form, and I believe verbally. You really need to move on."

"You failed to kill an enemy of the Institute when you had the chance. You used the Institute's lumen stone to steal gold from a dragon. Do you know what Grand Master Savus would do to you if he knew about that?"

"Decapitation with an iron sword?" He talked about that a lot.

"Worse." Shadows thickened around us, and the temperature dropped. My breath misted in front of my face at the chill in the air.

He took another step closer, and I shivered. "If you anger Grand Master Savus any further, the Shadow Fae will exalt you."

My eyebrows shot up. "Exalt? That doesn't sound bad. Exalt is a good thing, right?"

He shook his head. "In English, yes. I was using the Ancient Fae word. It's an execution method involving evisceration with burning iron instruments."

I winced. So I wasn't on the kill list, but it didn't sound like the situation was wonderful.

I let out a long, slow breath. Best not to piss him off more than I already had. "I get it. I'm sorry. I just had some responsibilities to take care of." Namely, Ciara. I didn't want to bang on about her though, in case I found the Institute using her as leverage, just as Baleros had.

His dark eyes lightened to violet once more, and his features softened, just a little. He stared at me for an uncomfortably long time before responding again. "I will send someone to collect your human."

He really did have a way with words.

He stalked off again, and I picked up my pace to follow after him.

"What happened to the trials after I left the Institute?"

"Training."

"For two months?" I asked, incredulous. I let out a sigh. "I guess it makes sense. Savus clearly has a favorite, doesn't he? He wants Maddan to win. Too bad extra training won't help that idiot."

Silence.

"I take it my return to the Institute won't be a warm welcome."

Silence.

"Can I kill Maddan during one of the trials?"

"Savus would likely exalt you if you did."

"That's the bad kind of exalting, right?"

"He'd send every Shadow Fae from every institute in the

world after you." Ruadan's rich voice rumbled through my gut. "Not to mention his mist army."

I grimaced. "I heard about the mist army. Melusine said he acquired it by killing the last Grand Master."

"Yes. And the point is, Maddan's death would cost the Institute millions of pounds per year."

I frowned. "Seems that no matter what I do, Savus wants to kill me. Why is he allowing me back into the Institute at all?"

"Because the Old Gods demand it. Choosing new Shadow Fae is their role. It's up to the Grand Master to interpret their desires."

As we moved closer to the Institute, my breath caught at the sight of the gleaming spires, light beaming into the night sky.

I quirked a smile. I imagined it would *really* piss off some of the fae nobility if the Old Gods favored a gutter fae ex-gladiator like me.

CHAPTER 3

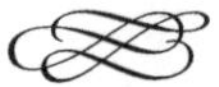

Trailing behind Ruadan, I crossed the threshold into a vaulted chamber within the Institute. Here, the ceiling arched high above us like the spine of a great beast. Floral vines climbed the stone, and moonlight shone in through peaked windows. I'd never been in this room before.

It was 3:30 in the morning, and the entire Institute had shown up to watch my return. A long stone aisle led to Grand Master Savus's throne, where the regal fae sat, a spindly silver crown gleaming on his head. A heavy mist curled around him, spooling from his fingertips. Guards flanked him on either side, each gripping an iron axe. My chest tightened at the sight of them.

The throne jutted from a stone floor, the back of it peaked like a second crown, glittering with dark jewels.

The other Shadow Fae lined the aisle. Aengus shot me a sharp look, his emerald eyes piercing—perhaps a bit irritated that I'd stabbed his friend.

But it wasn't just the knights in attendance. The two remaining novices stood there as well.

Maddan—that prick—was wearing a gold crown over his

autumn leaves and ginger hair. Lest anyone forget, he was a prince. He'd royally screwed up our last mission, stabbed me with a reaping dagger, and attempted to send me to the void, but that was fine. His father was a king, after all, and he had a pretty crown.

Given that Ruadan was characteristically silent all the way over here, I had no idea what I was in store for now. I only knew that the smug look on Maddan's face meant it wouldn't be pretty.

I followed a few paces behind Ruadan, crossing closer to Grand Master Savus. A phantom wind whispered through the hall, bringing up goosebumps on my skin.

In fact, the only friendly face in this hall was Melusine's. She flicked a strand of blue hair out of her eyes, and flashed me a wary smile. She actually looked nervous for me. Also not a great sign.

When we were just five feet from the throne, Ruadan abruptly stopped.

Savus's eyes flashed, and he leaned forward. "Kneel." Venom laced his voice.

Baleros had enforced his authority in exactly the same way, in grand public displays. The sharp reminder of Baleros had my blood racing. That man loved nothing more than making a spectacle of his authority. Inwardly, my mind was raging. For just a moment, I envisioned myself ripping the spray deodorant and lighter out of my bug-out bag and greeting Grand Master Savus with a makeshift flamethrower.

But in a room full of Shadow Fae, the glory of that moment would not last long, and I suppressed the impulse. Most importantly, I needed to stay alive to make sure Ciara got fed. After all, Ruadan had promised someone would fetch my human, hadn't he?

My stomach rumbled as I knelt on the cold stone floor. I

was freezing in my soaked dress.

"Novice." Savus's deep voice rang off the high ceilings. "I wanted to run your body full of iron nails, or perhaps give you some time in the iron maiden. We haven't exalted anyone in a while, and I was beginning to miss the spectacle of it."

My chest tightened. I hadn't expected hugs and margaritas, but this was a little bleaker than I'd anticipated.

"But your mentor persuaded me not to," he continued. "He explained that you went temporarily insane from the reaping dagger." For just a moment, his pale gaze flicked to Maddan. "And of course, your proximity to all the incubus magic drove you mad, and you found yourself wandering the streets of London, trying to satiate your lust—until Ruadan found you again."

That was what Ruadan had told them? I shot the Wraith a sharp look, but the shadows around him had thickened so intensely that I could hardly see him. Just his violet eyes in clouds of dark magic.

"Your mentor," Savus went on, "failed to control you."

For just a moment, I felt a twinge of guilt for getting Ruadan in trouble, before reminding myself that I did not care.

"More importantly," Savus's voice boomed over the hall, "you have made me question if allowing female novices was a mistake. Or perhaps allowing those of your social class. Maybe our predecessors had a good reason for excluding your kind." Ice laced his voice.

He was talking to me, but staring at Ruadan. Why? Did Savus have a problem with mongrels like us? I didn't entirely understand what the situation was, but given the tension crackling between the two male fae, I was starting to get the distinct impression that they were not on the same page.

Savus's gaze slid back to me, and he tapped his fingertips together.

"Because it seems that the Old Gods have favored you so far, we have removed you from the kill list. I put the trials on hold while you were away, communing with the Old Gods to divine their will. It seems they wanted your return. Assuming no one else stabs you with a reaping dagger, perhaps your skills could be of value to the Old Gods. If you can win the next three trials, I will continue to assume they favor you. If you fail any of the trials, then you will die a slow and painful death. Unfortunately, you have missed a bit of training. Oh well."

Maddan's eyes were fixed straight ahead, but his face was beaming. He was looking forward to my "slow and painful death." On my knees, I felt a hot flash of fury when I looked at him. He was a prince, and that meant he could get away with anything.

"However, the Institute does not tolerate insubordination. If you defy us, at some point, the favor of the Old Gods will turn against you. I had warned all the novices that you could not lose the lumen stone, or you would be executed with an iron axe. You chose to steal it from us." Something in his smile reminded me of a cat eyeing its prey. "I can hardly let you just waltz back in here to rejoin our ranks, can I?"

The stone floor bit into my knees as I knelt, and my fingers curled into fists. I wanted to say that I'd never asked for any of this. During the years when supernaturals were ferried off to the magical realms, I'd been locked in a cage. I'd emerged into a world where I was breaking the law just by existing.

Savus leaned back in his throne. "It's clear to me that you must be punished. Your new lodgings will be in the Palatial Room. If you are able to win every trial, we will reconsider your value, and perhaps you will even find a place here, after serving your penance. However, I find it hard to believe the Old Gods will favor you for long."

The Palatial Room? That didn't sound awful, but based on the delighted look on Maddan's face, I had to wonder what it meant.

I glanced at Ruadan. Even through the whorls of his dark magic, I could tell that his body had tensed.

General Savus lifted his skull cup. "Ruadan, please divest her of the lumen stone. We don't want her running away again, do we?"

Shadows billowed around Ruadan, and in the next moment, he was towering over me. His powerful hands clamped around my biceps, and he pulled me up from the floor—much more roughly than he needed to. Then, he reached for the lumen stone around my neck and yanked it off in a single, smooth motion.

When I glanced at Maddan and Melusine, I saw the violet stones gleaming around their necks.

This was, frankly, a load of shit. I was supposed to compete against the two other novices in the trials, without the benefit of a lumen stone. If I lost any of the trials, I'd be ripped apart with hot pincers.

I gritted my teeth. "This is a death sentence. Why drag it out?"

Savus nodded at one of the guards, and he started moving toward me with his axe.

My heart skipped a beat, and I held up my hand. "Wait! Okay. I'll do it. I'll join the trials without the lumen stone."

"I'm glad you came to your senses," said Savus. "Now, your mentor will escort you to your new lodgings. And Ruadan—along the way, please help our prisoner to understand the severity of her infractions."

Ruadan gripped my arm, but I jerked it away from him,

shooting him a ferocious look. He hadn't said much on the way here, but I still felt misled. "What about Ciara? You told me you'd send for my human."

"Did he say that?" an icy rage burned in Savus's eyes. What the hells was going on between these two?

Ruadan was gripping my arm again, his fingers tightening on my bicep. "It was the only way the gutter fae would come willingly. The simplest way to get her here without causing a scene."

I stared at him, white-hot fury simmering in my chest. So I was just *the gutter fae* now? And he'd misled me about Ciara. "I should have used the iron knife," I hissed through gritted teeth.

I couldn't bring myself to leave Ciara on her own. But what leverage did I have here?

My gaze flicked between Ruadan and Savus. They'd brought me here for a reason, hadn't they? Ruadan could have easily killed me, but they needed me to compete in the trials. Apparently, the Old Gods demanded it.

Leverage. Something Baleros had taught me to identify in every situation.

I straightened, staring at Savus. "If you want me to compete in your trials, instead of simply slaughtering your little prince over there, you will need to bring Ciara to the Institute. My human. I need to know that she is safe and taken care of."

Savus narrowed his eyes. "Do you really think you're in a position to make demands?"

"You need something from me, don't you? So it would seem that I am."

Savus tapped his silver hand on the stony armrest of his throne, considering me. "Fine. She'll join you in the dungeons. Find a separate cell for the human."

My stomach churned, and I was quickly getting the impression that my grim life as a gladiator had returned. At least Ciara and I would be together.

Ciarianna would rise again.

CHAPTER 4

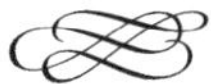

Ruadan dragged me down a dank set of stairs—dark stone faintly glistening in the candlelight. Down here, the dungeon air felt heavy with dirt and mildew.

Maybe it was my overactive imagination, but I thought I could hear the distant sounds of screaming. Was this where they tortured rogue supernaturals, or was someone just losing her mind in the darkness and isolation down there?

We reached a lower level, where fae guards stood within the shadows, iron swords and axes glinting in the faint light. They wore gloves to hold the hilts so that they wouldn't burn their hands—but one swing of those would be the end of me.

"When you said someone would fetch my human," I snarled, "you didn't mention she'd be imprisoned."

Ruadan said nothing.

"If I'd known these were the conditions," I said, "I'd have done my best to kill you. You're going to lock me in a cage. How very Baleros of you."

Ruadan jerked to a halt and turned to look at me. Shadows pooled in his eyes. Something about that comment was getting to him. And being who I was, I had an overwhelming impulse to stick the knife in further, to twist it a little. I had to know what enraged Ruadan.

Knowledge is power…

I was keenly aware that the guards were watching me, and that my time down here might be worse if I insulted one of their precious knights. And yet I couldn't quite restrain my desperate need to understand how he thought. What set him off? What were his limits? And most importantly, what was his deal with Baleros? Because that tension went *deep.*

"Very Baleros indeed," I said. "Dirt floor. A captive. Mind games. Sometimes you're nice to me. Sometimes you're throwing me into a medieval dungeon. Using kindness to manipulate. I think I've played this game before. Of course it makes sense. Baleros was one of you. You're all the same, I'm sure. Have you ever heard the theory that what people hate the most in others is what they hate in themselves? You are the mirror image of him."

Ruadan's fingers tightened on my bicep, and the chilling, demonic look on his features made ice run through my blood. But I wasn't done.

With my free hand, I tapped my lips. "He wasn't your father. He's not an incubus. So that means…he was your mentor."

A low growl from Ruadan confirmed my theory.

"Tell me, Ruadan. Did he ever keep you in the dungeons? Did he ever make you happy with little gifts? Sweets wouldn't do it for you, I'm sure. Praise, wasn't it? Did he give you praise every now and then to control you? Did he make you feel like he was your father and you needed his love, and then he turned on you?"

The guards were staring at us. Ruadan gripped my arm so tightly I thought he might break it. Then he started moving again, dragging me behind him. He picked up his pace, moving in a blur of speed, too fast for me to keep up without the lumen stone. I ran, but he was inhumanly fast. Soon my feet were dragging on the floor, my body bumping over the stone.

Was there a time when I thought Ruadan actually liked me? That he'd healed me and made me comfortable because he cared about how I felt? Obviously, I'd been an idiot.

Ruadan had been trained by Baleros, and the two men were probably more alike than I'd been willing to admit.

At the end of a passage, Ruadan flung open an iron-barred door. It creaked open to reveal a minuscule space.

My stomach dropped when I looked inside. This wasn't just a cage. This was *worse* than a cage. A cell too small to lie down in—one where I'd be stuck in a contorted position, crouching on the floor. *This* was the Palatial Room.

My breathing quickened. I didn't fear much, but tight spaces weren't my favorite. That was the legacy of six years in an underground tunnel—plus time locked in a box when Baleros wanted to punish me. I snarled at Ruadan, overcome by a desire to rip his pretty throat out.

He shoved me in, and my body slammed against the wall. I turned back to him, desperate to come up with a witty retort, something to let him know this wasn't getting to me. I wanted him to know that he couldn't affect me, that I felt no sense of betrayal, that I'd never expected anything from him in the first place. Except, tears stung my eyes, and my throat seemed to have closed.

I already felt the walls tightening in on me, and my mouth opened and closed without a single word on my tongue. His eyes had returned to their vibrant violet shade—no longer on the verge of killing. For the briefest of instants, I thought I saw a glimmer of sadness. Then, he slammed the cell door shut, and shadows consumed him as he stalked away.

I started to grip the bars, but as soon as I did, my fingertips burned. Of course. Iron.

My dress was still soaked from my little dip in the river, and I shivered. By the time I emerged from the Palatial Room for my next trial, I'd be completely filthy. Not to mention the fact that I had an unbelievable urge to pee, and the Palatial Room did not contain a toilet.

In the cramped space, my breath was coming in short, sharp bursts. It was only a few feet square, and I could hardly even sit. I definitely couldn't lie down, and I had to draw my knees up to my chest. At least I could see through the iron bars. Without that faint flicker of torchlight, I'd lose my mind.

But as I leaned back against the wall, I realized I was still wearing my bug-out bag. A smile started to curl my lips. Maybe I'd rattled Ruadan so much that he forgot to pull it off me.

My bag contained sweets, a now broken headlamp, lighters, soap, medical supplies, knives…and I had at least one bottle of water, which I could drink slowly to ration it. When I emptied it, I'd pee into it so I didn't have to sit in my own filth the whole time. Given that the door was iron, I wouldn't be able to get myself out of the cell, but I could improve my conditions at least a little.

Had Ruadan really overlooked that? I clenched my jaw.

Probably. I wasn't going to make the idiotic mistake again of thinking he'd been *nice* to me.

Still, I was pleased with his mistake. Maybe my time here wouldn't be so terrible, after all.

* * *

As Maddan stood before my cell, my mind went back to the time when I thought this wouldn't be so terrible. It seemed like days ago, but I had an awful feeling it had been something like twenty minutes. I was pretty familiar with how underground-cage time worked. Three days of underground-cage time was roughly twenty minutes in the real world. Hence, I was something like six thousand years old in cage years. Not sure of the exact math, as calculations weren't my strong point—particularly when sitting in a cell confronted by The Royal Fae Arsehole, and the unsettling sight of magic flicking between his fingertips.

Guards stood nearby. If Maddan murdered me right now, would they do anything to stop it? Probably not. After all, his father was a king and a benefactor, and it would save the Institute from the unpleasant possibility that the Old Gods might like me.

Maddan cocked his head, and red light gleamed between his fingers. At least he wasn't about to hit me with lust magic again, but I couldn't imagine the red magic would be pleasant.

CHAPTER 5

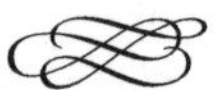

A dark smile curled Maddan's lips. "When I last saw you, you had the audacity to reject me. I slammed you with lust magic. Do you remember?"

Was there anything worse than a man who felt entitled to every woman he met? A man who would literally kill over a rejection? I thought of the iron knives in my bug-out bag. I could probably nail him with one right now.

Unfortunately for me, that would most definitely result in my death. I could kill him, yes, but there was no way out of this cell, and Savus had already made it clear that he mostly wanted to torment me a bit, then kill me in the most painful possible way.

So I would have to do something extremely difficult for me. Something that, had I ever seen a therapist, I would surely have been working on: not using violence as a way of getting out of every difficult situation.

Maddan cocked his head, the smug look on his face stoking my rage. "Am I right to understand that all the incubus magic drove you mad? That you roamed London's streets, satiating your lust in every filthy back alley until you wore yourself out?"

The story wasn't true, but I'd go with it anyway. He wanted denials, shame, and humiliation. He wouldn't get it.

"That's right. Every back alley. Lots of men." I looked at my fingers. Already, dirt had become encrusted under my nails. "I had a blast. Am I to understand that you're trying to make that sound like a bad thing? If your dead barguest friend had done the same, banging women all over London until he wore himself out, you'd have sung his praises. Don't you think?"

He cleared his throat, and I had the distinct impression that I'd taken the wind out of his sails. "You're still a whore."

I rolled my eyes. "Good one. And they say the royal fae have become stupid through centuries of inbreeding…"

The magic between his fingertips burned brighter. "You cannot talk to me like this, gutter fae. You try to humiliate me, over and over again."

And here we were at the crux of his problem. His giant ego. "You mean, when I kicked your arse at one trial after another, or when I said I found you repulsive?"

"A gutter fae, rejecting a prince…" he snarled.

He hurled the magic at me, and it slammed into me through the iron bars. Pain spread through my body, racking my bones. I started shaking, fingers wildly clutching at the stone walls, trying to manage the agony. My mind flashed to the knives in my bag, and I was doing everything in my power not to pull one out right then and throw it at him.

Don't kill the prince. Don't kill the prince. Don't kill the prince.

When I looked up at Maddan again, I was gritting my teeth. "What do you hope to accomplish here, prince? When the next trial comes up, they will be unleashing me on the world. And I might not be gentle when I take you down."

He didn't respond, just summoned another flash of red

fire and threw it at me. I raised my arms to block it, but it slammed into my forearms, and the pain raced through my bones, my tendons, ripping me apart. I grunted, trying to keep myself from screaming. I didn't know what this magic was—if it was actually breaking my bones, or if it just delivered pain. Either way, by the time I got to the next trial, I may not be in the condition to take him down at all.

Another blast of his hellish magic tore through my body, and I could no longer think straight. The pain was splintering. A few disconnected thoughts flickered in my mind—Maddan is a prick...Ruadan is a prick...Savus is a prick... Nothing particularly useful or insightful.

With the final attack—one last burst of red magic—I fell back against the wall, and my world began to go dark.

* * *

I BREATHED in the scent of apples. I felt rough stone biting into my back where I leaned against the wall, and as I gasped for breath, I felt particles of dirt going into my lungs. But the air smelled different now. It smelled of the city of Emain, and in my mind's eye, I could see the apple trees dappling the mythical land's wild hills.

Pain racked my body, and I groaned. Gentle fingers lifted me from the stone until I was standing, my eyes still closed from fatigue. I slumped into a powerful body. Apples and pine.

My mouth had gone completely dry, and I licked my lips. "Who's there?" I asked, still half asleep, even though I knew by his scent it was Ruadan.

"It's me." He whispered so quietly, I almost didn't hear him.

My eyes snapped open, and I found myself staring at the dark contours of a shirt. Then, I looked up into violet eyes, bright in the darkness. His powerful arms held me up, and heat radiated from his body over my freezing skin. I hated the bastard, but despite myself, I wanted him to stay here with his arms wrapped around me, just for the warmth.

The Palatial Room offered barely enough space for two people to stand—especially given the size of Ruadan's broad shoulders. He pulled me closer to him, his muscled body pressing against me. I was dimly aware that I still stank of river water and piss, but I was too tired to care. In fact, I was glad Ruadan had to deal with the stench.

"Where's Ciara?" I asked in a whisper.

He leaned down, and his breath warmed the shell of my ear. "She's here. Two cells down. You must be quiet."

"Why are you here?" I whispered.

He put his finger over my lips, shushing me. Interesting. He didn't want the guards knowing he was in here.

I felt the warmth of his fingertips on the small of my back, and he traced up my spine. Healing magic pulsed in my body, comforting and soothing. One of his enormous hands encircled my waist. As much as I hated it, my skin was warming in response to his incubus magic.

His fingertips traced higher up my spine, and the pain flowed out of my body.

When his hand stroked down my back again, an unwelcome memory bloomed in my mind—me, naked in Ruadan's bed, writhing against him.

What the fuck was wrong with me? My body was in complete rebellion against my better judgment. It was the incubus magic.

Ruadan leaned down, whispering, "You need to survive."

Before I could look up into his eyes again, his cold magic pulsed over my body. Silently, he opened the iron gate, and disappeared into the prison's shadows. He was gone.

I leaned back against the rough wall, the stones cutting

into my skin through my dress. My muscles and bones still ached, but not nearly as much as before. I slid down the stones, grimacing a bit.

The fucker hadn't even bothered to heal me all the way. He could have, but I supposed he needed to heal me just enough so I wouldn't expire before the trials. He wanted me punished as much as Savus did, but he also wanted to make sure I lived.

Crammed into the Palatial Room, I leaned back against the cell wall.

The dim torchlight wavered over something on the floor that made my heart leap in my chest.

A butterscotch sweet.

My mouth went dry. Baleros, my old gladiator master, had used a butterscotch to control me with a glimmer of kindness. But he was dead now.

Right?

For a moment, I wondered if it was real at all, or just my mind screwing with me. Then, I reached for it, picking it up with a shaking hand. I felt as if Baleros were fucking with me, except he was dead. Had Ruadan left this here? Why would he try to mess with me like that?

With a snarl, I threw the butterscotch out of my cell, between the bars.

It took a few minutes of deep breathing before I could relax myself, forcing my heartbeat to slow.

"Ciara?" I called out into the darkness, and my voice echoed off the rocks.

Only a faint dripping noise answered.

"Ciara?" I tried again.

"I'm here," she said. "You know, I think we were a little better off in Ciarianna Castle."

"In what?"

"The burnt-out car. I've started calling it Ciarianna Castle in my mind, even though I kept finding myself sleeping on eggshells and half-eaten chicken bones. But that seems like paradise now. Here, I have to sleep on bugs and dead mice, just like I did as a little girl. But I'm not going to let them get to me. I'm beating the system."

"How, exactly?"

"I'm not going to sleep on bugs, because I'm not going to sleep. I've been keeping myself awake by standing."

I held my head in my hands. "You need to get some sleep, Ciara. Human brains break if you don't sleep."

"That's a myth. Like, there are a lot of benefits to permanent wakefulness…you have more time for thinking, and you start to hear voices. Worst-case scenario, you get visual hallucinations, possibly permanent brain damage." Her voice echoed off the rocks.

"Ciara. I'm going to get us out of here."

"Or maybe I'll get us out of here," she said. "Did you know that the women in my family are legendary protectors? Fiery. Like demons. Family legend says my grandma came from a flaming pit under the Appalachian Mountains. Grandma McDougall was a fearsome woman. She caught squirrels for breakfast with her bare hands, snapped their necks. She wore gowns of raccoon fur and crowns of black locust leaves, and men trembled before her."

I wasn't entirely sure if this was an actual family legend or the product of her prison hallucinations.

"Well," I said, "maybe you'll get us out of here."

"The McDougalls protect people we love. So you'd better believe I won't let anything happen to you. When it comes down to it, I will protect you with everything I've got. I come from mountain fire."

"Okay, sweetie. Close your eyes."

"Ciarianna will rise again. And when she does, she will

light her enemies on fire. She will glory in their screams and bathe in their ashes."

For a sweet woman who got excited about things like "bologna cake," Ciara could be remarkably macabre.

"Ciarianna will dance on their graves," I added.

"She will fashion flutes and other wind instruments out of their bones. And then she will celebrate their demise with a meal of Twinkies."

The dripping of water filled the silence. "You kind of frighten me sometimes, you know that, Ciara? Maybe just... settle down a little."

"You can't trust these people at the Institute. Ruadan is a pretty man with a face like a god, but you don't know jack about him."

"Oh, believe me. I know."

"Things aren't always what they seem. The devil wears many—"

The slamming of metal against metal cut her off. "Shut it, you two!" boomed a male voice. "Or I'll cut your tits off."

I gritted my teeth. When I got out of here, I was going to punch that guy in the dick.

"Ciara," I loudly whispered. "Ciarianna will rise again."

Time for me to rest a little. Slowing my breathing, I leaned my head against the sludgy rock, and then willed myself to sleep.

CHAPTER 6

I crouched in the cell. I had no idea how much time had passed. Two days, perhaps? I only knew that Maddan never returned, and that one of the guards had shoved water and gruel through the cell's trapdoor around four or five times.

But worst of all, every time I fell asleep, I'd wake to find another butterscotch in my cell. And each time I found one, I'd hurl it out from between the bars.

Somehow, I'd managed to sleep most of the time in the cell—dreaming of Emain the whole time. I did my best to ration out the sweets from my bag—lollipops, two chocolate bars, a bag of peppermints. Proper athlete stuff. I'd be in amazing shape by the time I had to fight anyone.

In the middle of a particularly delicious dream of Emain, one in which I was biting into a sweet apple, the sound of my name snapped me out of my sleep.

I woke, blinking in surprise at the sight of Melusine standing outside my cell.

She held a little bundle in her hands—something

wrapped in cloth—and she shoved it through the cell bars, wincing as her hand brushed against the iron.

"What are you doing here?" I asked.

"I brought you food. I see a dungeon, I think hunger. I put two and two together. I've got to tell you though, it was not easy getting in here. I had to give the guards a sleep potion, and they're already stirring."

I blinked, snatching up the little bundle. "I was starting to think everyone had forgotten about me."

She shook her head. "No one has. Maddan keeps talking about you. All the time. I think he's obsessed with you. When I hear someone talking about the same thing all the time, I think 'obsessed.' I put two and two together. Ruadan has been stalking around, snarling at everyone, like he wants to rip off everyone's head. I see black eyes on a demon, and I think 'anger.' I can't say why, but I think it has to do with you."

I shook my head. "What happens if Savus defies the Old Gods?"

"The Old Gods have blessed Savus with the silver crown that gives him power of the Institute. As long as he has their blessing, no one can take that thing off. No one can kill him or overthrow him, or challenge his power. The Old Gods bestow their blessing on novices. They make the choice, and the Grand Master is just supposed to interpret it. If you keep winning in the trials, it means the Old Gods favor you. If Savus gets rid of you, he'd be going against their will. He could lose the crown. Anyone could depose him. Ruadan especially. I see them snarling at each other, I think they're angry at each other. Competing like stags. Know what I mean?"

Ahh…so I had some serious leverage. Savus needed me to keep his power within the Institute. In fact, maybe the Old

Gods would be my ticket out of the Palatial Room of Nightmares.

"This is extremely valuable information, Melusine. Maybe even my way out of here." A rock was digging into one of my shoulder blades, and I winced, rubbing the raw flesh. "I guess the 'Palatial Room' is something of a Shadow Fae joke."

She blinked at me. "Fae nobility don't make jokes. They're incapable of it. *Palatial* is actually an Ancient Fae word, translating to something in English like..." she scratched her cheek as she thought.

"The devil's arsecrack?" I offered.

"Festering dung-hole would be more accurate."

"I see. That is quite accurate."

Someone groaned farther down the hallway, and Melusine touched the violet lumen stone at her neck. "They're already waking. I've got to go."

"Wait!" I said, maybe a little too loud. I thrust the bundle of food back at her, grimacing at the sting from the iron bars. "Can you give this to Ciara?"

She nodded once and snatched the food from me. My stomach rumbled and my mouth watered at the scent of food, but at least I'd had a few sweets to sustain me. Ciara had nothing but gruel the whole time. Plus, I'd had the pleasure of dreaming of apples and baked bread.

Melusine frowned at the food, then nodded again. Shadows burst around her, and she disappeared.

Gods, I missed my lumen stone. If I ever got out of this prison alive, I'd be stealing it back.

I took a deep breath, my eyes already growing heavy. Why was I so tired?

"Ciara?" I called out.

"Yeah?"

"Are you okay there?"

"Someone just dropped off a package—"

"Shhhhh. I know." I desperately wanted to know what was in it. Chicken? Bread? I clutched my famished stomach. At this point, I'd start eating the gruel.

"I'm going to get us out of here," I promised.

I picked up another butterscotch from the dirt floor, and threw it out from between the bars.

"Ciara." I loosed a long breath. "I keep finding butterscotches." She would know what that meant.

"Who's leaving them? It's not *you-know-who.* He's dead, Arianna."

"I know. But I have no idea where they're coming from."

"Maybe Ruadan. Not sure that I trust the man. Not sure that I trust shadows and darkness." She was talking with her mouth full, and my stomach rumbled again. "The devil wears many faces."

"I know."

"I said that shadowy monster—"

Metal slammed against metal again, and a guard's voice barked, "What did I tell you?"

"Right. You'll cut our tits off," I said. Sometimes, men were the worst.

* * *

ROUGH HANDS JERKED me out of another dream of Emain.

Someone was yanking me up, and I blinked at the sight of the open cell door.

It took me a moment to realize that Ruadan had returned, and that he was dragging me out of my cell. He wasn't exactly gentle about it.

He dragged me past Ciara's cell, and I caught a quick glimpse of her slumbering against the wall, covered in crumbs. The sight warmed my heart.

I scrambled for balance, then elbowed him hard in the chest. "You don't have to drag me everywhere. Arsehole. I can walk."

"Your next trial begins soon," he said. "You'll need to be cleaned and fed if you're going to pass it."

"Cleaned and fed? You're making me sound like a farm animal."

"Well, no one knows what your other half is. It's entirely possible."

I glared at him. Was that a…joke? No. Fae nobility didn't make jokes. He was just a twat.

Still, I didn't *hate* the idea of taking a bath and eating a proper meal.

As I passed the guards, one of them sniffed the air, his lip curling in disgust. In cage years, I'd been in there for, I don't know, decades? But given the number of meals I'd received so far, I'd wager it had been something like three days. Three days during which my competition had been preparing, while I'd been eating lollipops for sustenance and getting my bones broken by magic.

Ruadan let go of my arm, and I started to wonder how difficult it would be to simply escape on the next task. Could Savus really hunt me down and exalt me? The hardest part would be getting Ciara out of here.

"What is the next trial, exactly?" I asked.

"You'll do fine."

"You didn't answer my question." I followed him up the narrow stairwell, my muscles burning. I'd been in a contorted position for far too long—not to mention the fact that I still hadn't fully healed from Maddan's magical assault. "I probably will do fine, but what is the task? If I screw anything up, I'll literally be torn to pieces."

"The next trial involves killing vampires using a stake. I'll be with you the entire time, so you won't be able to escape. Without the lumen stone, you are slow and sluggish."

Slow and sluggish? "Remember when you couldn't talk? I'm thinking fondly of those days."

I knew that I stank like the bottom of a sewer, but I was angry enough at Ruadan that I felt satisfied he had to deal with the stench.

When we reached the sunlight, it burned my eyes, and I lifted an arm to shield my vision. I sort of wanted to crawl into a coffin. So *this* is how vampires felt.

I blinked in the bright light as my eyes adjusted. "Are we going to your room?"

"You're not going anywhere near my room."

"Just because I put a little knife in your heart? Honestly. You're all making a big deal out of nothing." I shadowed my eyes as we crossed the flowery green. After the magical beating I'd taken, I could hardly keep up with Ruadan, and I walked with a limp. "Does anyone else know about…my time in the arena?"

"No."

Interesting. He wasn't entirely forthcoming with Grand Master Savus.

We reached the tower door, and Ruadan opened it into the stairwell.

My bones ached, and I glared at him. "You didn't heal me very well."

He shot me a sharp look, then gave a subtle shake of his head. He wanted me to drop it.

As Ruadan and I walked up the stairs, anger started to simmer in my chest. Ruadan had drastically misled me when he'd lured me here. "You never said anything about a prison cell. And I distinctly remember a promise that someone would fetch my human."

"The promise was honored," he said.

"But you threw her in a dungeon. She would have been better off where she was." Fury was rising now. I suppressed the urge to punch him hard in his beautiful face and mess it up a little. "You are no different than Baleros, who I'd vowed to kill. Are you so certain you'll outlive me?" The words exploded out of me, and I knew I was being incautious, but after days in the Palatial Room, I didn't have the best grip on self-restraint. Plus, my body still ached from Maddan's attack, and a wild hunger was making me feel a little crazy.

Ruadan simply fell silent, and he led me down the hall until we reached an oak door.

He pushed it open, revealing a sparse stone bathroom. Like the other bathrooms I'd seen at the Institute, the stone tub seemed to grow from the flagstone floor itself like a natural feature. The bath had already been filled. Ruddy sunlight streamed in through the window, blazing through the curls of steam that rose from the bathtub. While the bath itself looked inviting, I wasn't super thrilled at the sight of six armed fae guards standing around the room, staring at the tub. Were they going to watch me bathe?

"I'm supposed to bathe in here?" I asked.

"You will need to be clean for your next trial. You're going to infiltrate a vampire's den, and you'll need to blend in. The filth on your body would make it difficult." He raised his eyes to the guards. "Turn around."

"But sir," one of them began, "Savus has ordered—"

"Turn around." The cold fury in his voice brooked no argument. "And if I catch you looking at her, I will sever your head from your body before you can draw another breath."

CHAPTER 7

"Aren't you the gentleman," I said drily. "You leave me in a festering dung hole where my enemies can torture me within an inch of my life. But gods forbid anyone sees my nipples." Fae males were absurd. Possibly all males were absurd.

The shadows around Ruadan grew so thick, they seemed to suck all the air out of the room. With one last withering look, he turned away from me. With his back to me, he stood in the doorway, his large frame blocking my exit. Weapons glinted all over his body—knives strapped to his legs, the sword on his back. Every inch of him was equipped to kill, while I was about to strip myself completely naked. The balance of power was not in my favor here, if I wanted to cause trouble.

I surveyed the room. There wasn't much in here, except a short wooden table with some clothing and a towel.

I looked down at my dress. At one point, it had been white, but now dirt smeared the fabric—along with a few red smudges from what I thought were my sweets (or perhaps blood), and green stains that I thought might be from moss or mildew growing in the Palatial room. In short, I was absolutely disgusting.

I breathed in deeply, determined to convince Ruadan that none of this was getting to me. "Do I *have* to bathe? I've been a bit nostalgic for the old days." He knew what I meant, even if the guards didn't: my cage underground. "Right now, I smell like home. You know what I mean, don't you?"

"Undress."

I blinked. Even with his back to me, even in a room full of guards, there was definitely something unmistakably sensual about that word on his tongue. "Clean yourself. Then, you will eat."

Despite his commanding tone, his voice seemed to wrap itself around my body, stroking places I desperately needed to wash right now. But I pushed his allure out of my mind. He was a monster—a devil wearing a beautiful face—and he'd *exalt* me on a whim if it struck his fancy.

"It's unfortunate you had to take me out of my Palatial Room. I was having the most exquisite dreams in there." I pulled off my dress and tossed it on the stone floor, then stepped out of my underwear. The drafty castle air whispered over my skin. "But do you know? Every now and then I'd think of you, Ruadan, and what a lovely man you are. Am I getting that word right—*lovely?* My Ancient Fae is rusty. I'm looking for something that translates to 'violet-eyed psycho twat' in English."

He didn't answer, but his body looked tightly coiled, like he was about to explode. What was that about?

I cocked my head. It was the same tension that had gripped his body when I lay in bed with him. He was supposed to be celibate. As an incubus, it couldn't be easy for him to be this close to a naked woman. Is that what it was about?

Like a child poking a bug with a stick, I wanted to prod at

that wound to see what would happen. "It feels good to get those filthy clothes off. I'm awfully dirty though, Ruadan. Perhaps you can help me bathe?"

His growl rumbled through my gut.

"It's just that there are some delicate places I can't quite reach on my own, and you're so good with your hands." I dipped one foot into the bath, sighing at the feel of warm water on my skin. "I do remember what your fingers felt like on my body when you healed me. I remember what it felt like when I was naked in bed with you, writhing—" I unleashed a long sigh. "Oh, that's right. You've taken a vow of celibacy. Never mind, then. How long has it been, anyway? Centuries? Is it true that Shadow Fae in other institutes are allowed to enjoy the pleasures of the flesh? Kissing, stroking, fucking up against the stone walls? Too bad you're in the one institute where none of that's allowed. Must be hard for an incubus. So to speak."

His magic thickened in the room, shadows darkening around him. I couldn't help but smile. I *was* getting to him, and it filled me with satisfaction.

Then, I stepped in, submerging myself completely in the stone tub. It felt amazing.

I pulled a bar of soap from the stone lip of the tub, and I began scrubbing some of the grime off my legs.

"If I become a knight, I'm not sure I'd be able to abide by that particular rule. The celibacy one. I suppose I could always pleasure myself in the bath."

"Stop talking," Ruadan snarled.

I smiled again as I ran the soap over my arms, watching the bath slowly fill with dirt from my body.

The fun in prodding at Ruadan was beginning to wear off, and I frowned as I washed myself. Why, exactly, were all the guards necessary? As Ruadan had so nicely pointed out, without a lumen stone on my body, I was slow and sluggish.

There was no way in hells I could escape someone who could shadow-leap. Why did they need six guards here if Ruadan could easily guard me on his own?

Maybe it had to do with the animosity between Savus and Ruadan. Maybe the Grand Master didn't want us speaking to each other. Perhaps they weren't here to guard me, but to report on Ruadan. After all, he'd tried to keep it a secret when he'd healed me in the cell, hadn't he?

I ran the soap under my filthy fingernails, getting dirt all over the soap. Why had Ruadan left me with the lumen stone I'd stolen?

Even if he was simply a violet-eyed shadow twat, his behaviors were confusing and inconsistent. He left me alive, left me with a lumen stone, campaigned to spare my life…He even concealed my connection to Baleros from the Institute. Then he dragged me into a prison and left me there. He healed me, but only a little.

At this point, I had no idea how to predict his actions or motivations, and he was a complete cipher. I needed to speak to him alone—except it seemed Savus didn't want that to happen.

I turned on the tap to wash my lavender hair, and quickly lathered up my locks. Then I bent under the tap to rinse myself. The stream of water ran brown with all the filth from my body. When I'd completely scrubbed my skin and hair, I unplugged the drain, letting the filthy water drain out. Then, I rinsed my entire body with fresh water from the tap. I sniffed my bicep, inhaling the smell of lavender. Completely pristine.

Utterly naked, I crossed to Ruadan, and I touched his back, watching his muscles tense as if I'd burned him. "I'm getting dressed now."

I crossed to the table, my bare feet padding over the cold floor and leaving wet footprints.

As I pulled on the fresh underwear, I stared at Ruadan's enormous back. "Do I get to learn anything else about the trial before we begin? Do I need magic?"

"You won't need magic," Ruadan answered. "Just to kill vampires. This clan happens to be particularly ancient and powerful, but I trust your ability to kill."

"I want to go to the library," I said. I pulled a tight, black dress over my head, finding that it fit my body perfectly.

"Why the library?" he asked. "You don't have much time."

"It's how I prepare." I needed no preparation to kill vampires. I just wanted to be alone with Ruadan for a few moments if I could get them.

One of the guards shifted in place. "Sir, Grand Master Savus ordered us to remain with you and the gutter fae at all times."

"It's just a quick trip to the library," I protested.

"I will take you for a few moments," said Ruadan.

"Sir," the guard said, "I don't believe we're supposed to deviate from—"

With an explosion of shadow magic, Ruadan whirled and slammed his fist into the wall just by the guard's head. Bits of rock rained down, and Ruadan glared into his eyes.

"Then come with us," Ruadan snarled. "So you can report to your Master that you've done your job."

My gaze flicked to the floor, where urine pooled at the guard's feet.

I crossed my arms, staring at Ruadan. Savus was old, and lacked Ruadan's demonic night magic powers. If it weren't for the magical power of the Old Gods, Ruadan would clearly be the alpha fae. Savus better hope he didn't piss off those gods.

* * *

We crossed into the library, my heart already warming at the smell of books, and the sight of library moths dusting the shelves. Glow worms, suspended by silk from the ceiling, cast golden light over crooked shelves of books.

As we crossed between two stacks, I caught a glimpse of my favorite librarian hovering on her magical Segway. Her silver hair seemed to float around her as she moved up and down.

I cast a quick glance back at the guard who was trailing us, his eyes locked on me. His skin had paled, and he clearly looked terrified at the prospect of having to choose between infuriating Savus or Ruadan.

The librarian zoomed around a corner, then screeched to a halt. She peered down over her moon-shaped spectacles. "Can I help you?"

"I'm looking for nonfiction vampire books," I said. "And if you happen to have a paper and pencil, I'm hoping to take some notes."

She reached into the pocket of her shimmering blue dress, and pulled out a little lined notepad and a pencil. She handed them to me.

"Thank you."

"Follow me." She nodded curtly, then zoomed across the library to an enormous archway, its shelves crammed full of books. I picked up my pace, hurrying to catch up with her. I swear she'd become even speedier since the last time I saw her. Reckless, even.

Ruadan didn't utter a word as we walked, and the fae guard simply stomped along behind us.

The librarian hovered just above us, high in the archway. She peered down at us, then gestured at one of the walls.

"Vampires," she declared.

My gaze roamed up and down the ancient books, and I randomly pulled one from the shelf, titled *The Vampyre.*

I glanced back at the guard, who was staring at us, his blue eyes narrowed. The librarian whooshed over our heads at a speed that made my heart race. It was a wonder that woman didn't injure herself.

Standing next to Ruadan, I cracked open the book, and began jotting down my "notes." I needed some answers.

Why did you heal me, but only partway?

He pointed at what I was writing. "You've got that wrong. Let me do it."

He snatched the notepad and pencil from me.

You need to appear injured. Don't trust anyone.

I loosed a long, slow breath. I was still confused, and I snatched the pencil back.

Why do I need to appear injured?

I heard the guard take another step behind me, and I slammed the book shut before he could see what we'd been writing.

The guard cleared his throat. "The trial begins soon, sir. Savus will exalt me if I defy his orders."

We'd never gotten around to that feeding part, and my stomach rumbled. And all I'd learned was that Ruadan was hiding things from the other Shadow Fae.

CHAPTER 8

We waited on a tiny street in London's Smithfield, illuminated by the amber glow of a streetlight. The air felt heavy and damp, as if rain were going to fall.

By ancient hospital walls, I stood between Melusine and Maddan. I smoothed out my clean black dress. On the way here, Ruadan had tossed me a chunk of stale bread. Better than nothing, I supposed. My bones and muscles still ached —but not nearly as much as they would if Ruadan hadn't healed me.

Maddan narrowed his eyes at me and growled. Considering what he'd done to me, he probably had no idea how I was standing at all.

I ignored him, instead focusing on my surroundings. Centuries ago, this had been a place of execution—the very place where William Wallace had died a horrific death, just outside a medieval hospital. The place also where Bloody Mary had burned the Protestants. Here, the scent of human death had mingled with the offal and refuse of the butchery trade.

We'd be bringing the death back to Smithfield in the form of another trial.

Seemed a perfect way to spend a Saturday night, I supposed. I wasn't entirely sure where we'd be going, but it was most likely the dark, medieval church on the other side of an ornate Tudor gate. It was the exact sort of creepy place a vampire would inhabit. They'd probably been in it for centuries.

Mist flowed over the ground, and the hair on my arms stood on end. The fog itself formed eerie shapes, as if it were alive—wolves, lions, grasping fingers. The sound of footfalls echoed off the stone. Then, Grand Master Savus crossed in front of us, his fingers steepled.

Thunder rumbled over the horizon, the boom skimming my skin.

Ruadan walked behind Savus, his dark magic tingeing the mist with shadows. Tonight, Ruadan was acting as my prison guard, making sure I didn't escape anywhere.

Savus's pale eyes bored into me. "You all know that you're supposed to silently enter and kill in the shadows. Do not do anything that calls attention to yourselves. Kill when no one is looking. As soon as the vampires learn that Shadow Fae have entered their lair, they will descend upon you and feast like vultures on a corpse."

I blinked innocently. "Anything attention-grabbing, like stabbing the other novices with a reaping dagger? Like hurling lust magic at them? That sort of thing?"

Savus didn't answer, but he continued glaring at me.

"Your task tonight is to enter their lair, and kill as many of the vampires as you can without the humans in their company realizing. This clan is at least five centuries old, and they believe London is their home. They are wrong. They should have fled for a magical realm years ago. We believe ten or fifteen vampires lurk in there. If you are capable of remaining in the shadows, you should be able to take them all on. If you are clumsy and expose your presence, you will all die."

I had a thin wooden stake jammed between my cleavage, which meant I had everything I needed to kill vampires. A simple hawthorn stake to the heart, and the vampires would be sent to the shadow void for all of eternity. Vampires weren't nearly as difficult to kill as Ruadan, and I'd killed plenty in the arena. The only tricky part would be the "stick to the shadows" directive. And maybe the first hurdle of getting into their lair.

In fact, I wasn't entirely sure how Savus expected me to get into the church. The others—including Ruadan—could simply shadow-leap wherever they wanted. I didn't have that advantage.

Still, my time in the arena had taught me how vampires thought. Most vampire males would welcome an innocent female, seeing us as fresh blood. All I had to do was knock and make sure they didn't notice the stake between my boobs, until it was too late.

My objectives tonight: kill vampires, find alone time with Ruadan so I could interrogate him before someone tried to throw me back in the filthy piss hole.

"Be warned," said Savus, "the vampires have been living in horrific, depraved conditions. What you find in there might be worse than you imagined."

For a moment, a shudder whispered up my spine, but I quickly mastered control of myself. How bad could it be? A bit of blood, some horrible skull decor? A severed head and some rotting limbs here and there? I'd practically grown up around carnage. It didn't scare me.

"Now." Something dark glinted in Savus's eyes. "Go out there and slaughter."

Melusine and Maddan were off before I took my first

step, shadow-leaping away. The flicker of movement by the old Tudor church gate told me they were slipping beneath its ancient arches into the cemetery. Heading for the medieval church, just as I'd thought.

For a moment, I considered rushing after them as fast as I could limp on my hobbled legs, but I reconsidered. Their departure had been a little too hasty. None of us knew for certain that the vampires were in the old gothic church—it just *seemed* vampy.

I stepped out of the shadows of St. Bartholomew's Hospital. I sniffed the air. Given all the shadow magic pulsing around us from Ruadan and the other novices, I couldn't use that to pick up the scent of vampires.

Thunder boomed again, lightning cracking the sky.

The muscles barked in my legs, and I limped down a narrow road near the church, noting the street sign—Little Britain. A light rain began to fall, dampening my black dress.

I sniffed the air again. Now, another smell hung in the air —one faint, but distinct. The coppery smell of human blood. I smiled. *That's* how I would track the vampires, and it wasn't coming from the church. I sniffed again, moving further down the narrow road. As I walked, Ruadan's magic whispered over my skin from behind me.

Lucky for me, I didn't need to depend on speed. As the scent of blood intensified, I was increasingly sure that the others had gone in the wrong direction.

I glanced behind me, irritated to find that Savus was staring at Ruadan and me from the mouth of the narrow street. I wouldn't be able to speak to Ruadan with the Grand Master watching.

I limped onward, until the scent of blood led me to a pub, the facade painted with chipped brown and green paint. The place looked like a bit of a dump, with empty crates piled out front, and a few half-drunk pints.

I could hardly make out the pub's name. I looked closely and saw that the faint gold lettering above the door read *The Garlic and Cross.* Those things were not actually repellent to vampires, but maybe it was an in-joke. In any case, the scent told me I was in the right place.

Then, to my utter horror, I noticed the hand-drawn, grammatically incorrect sign on the door. It heralded something I hoped I'd never have to encounter, something I'd spent years avoiding.

Saturday! Open Mic Night. Comedian's. Singer's. Performance art. £5.

I swallowed hard. Savus had been right. This *was* more depraved than I'd anticipated.

And on top of it all, I had no money to get in. I'd been living in a bloody dungeon.

I glanced at Ruadan. "I don't suppose you have a fiver?"

"I'm not allowed to help you. If the Old Gods favor you, then you will be able to succeed in the trials no matter what obstacles lie in your path."

"What exactly is the point of you?" I snapped.

He narrowed his eyes, his dark magic lashing the air around him. "I'm the only thing keeping you alive."

"What do you mean?"

His gaze slid back to Savus, who was lingering nearby, and he fell silent again.

The rain had begun to fall harder, soaking my hair, and I hugged myself. I didn't suppose I could simply kill the doorman. Might create a bit of a spectacle.

No, I'd have to blag my way into the bar, because there was no way in hells I was volunteering as a performer.

Now, the rain was really pouring down, soaking my clothing.

Baleros's fifteenth law of power: Always use your surroundings.

I glanced across the street at another pub—The Crown

and Two Chairmen. An idea started to form in my mind. I'd have to start there before I made my way into the vamp bar.

I ignored Ruadan's presence and pushed into the second pub. It was a Saturday night, and the place was completely full. Humans sat crammed around the old wooden tables, or lingered between them with pints. I could easily move unnoticed in here. I scanned the empty wineglasses and pints on the tables. Within moments, I was collecting them by the armful, acting like I worked in the place. If you appeared confident enough, no one questioned it.

When I'd stuffed my arms full of the glassware, I crept out into the rain with my stolen bounty.

Ruadan was waiting for me outside, his magic darkening the air. "What on Earth are you doing?"

"Finding a way in before Prince Fuckwit figures out what the hells he's doing." I let some rainwater fill the glasses, and then I dumped the remnants onto the street. Clean.

I snatched one of the old crates off the ground outside the pub—along with the pint glasses—and I crammed all the glassware into it. With a smile, I stood.

I pulled open the door to the pub to reveal a rickety stairwell, and Ruadan followed behind me.

I paused at the top of the stairs. As soon as the door creaked closed behind Ruadan, I turned to him. "Tell me what's going on. Why didn't you warn me about the prison cell?"

"I didn't know Savus was going to throw you in prison. And we don't have time to discuss this now. Savus will be watching us through a scrying mirror. I'm going to hide myself." His gaze sharpened. "Arianna, don't do anything stupid. You can't escape the Shadow Fae. Do you understand?"

"Yeah, I get it. I'm a prisoner. Understood."

Shadows bloomed around Ruadan, and he was gone without another word.

My jaw tightened, and I gripped my crate of glasses. Of course, Savus watched everything we did in the trials.

I limped down the creaking stairs, already cringing at the sound of stilted comedy booming through the club.

A human man sat at a desk at the bottom of the stairs, flicking through his mobile phone, utterly bored. When he saw me, he tapped his fingernails on the wood. "Five pounds, please, darling."

"Oh, I'm just here to deliver the glasses you wanted." I had once again lapsed into an American accent, which seemed to happen every time I wanted to blag my way into a nightclub. I honestly couldn't explain it.

He narrowed his eyes. "Someone asked for more glasses?"

If you acted confident enough, you could get away with anything.

"Yeah. The owner. Said you were running out." Standing tall, I began to step into the bar.

"Hang on," he grabbed my arm. "I'm the owner. What are you trying to pull?"

My jaw tightened.

Fuck it. Fuck it all to hells. I needed the Old Gods on my side, or I faced a grisly death.

I cleared my throat. "I meant to say, the glasses are part of my act. It's all…it's all part of my act. I'm here to perform."

CHAPTER 9

"Part of your act?" he repeated.

My pulse raced. "It's a glass-shattering act."

He stared at me. If I'd had a few more minutes to prepare, I probably would have come up with something a little more artistic than "glass-shattering." Maybe those people who make music with the rims of glasses, or maybe some kind of glass-related dance routine. But I was short on time, short on talent, and as usual, my first and most powerful instinct was simply to break things.

"It's totally a thing," I said in a voice suggesting that he was an idiot. "You haven't heard of glass shattering?" I crinkled my forehead. "It's huge in Brooklyn. You know, in New York. America." Overdoing it. Tone it down, Arianna.

He stroked his beard. "Of course I've heard of glass shattering." He nodded at the man on the stage—a pale-skinned fellow in a flouncy shirt. "After this prick is done, you're on. What's your name, darling?"

"Arianna."

The man on stage gripped his microphone. Long, black hair hung over his translucent skin, and I caught a flash of fangs. "So what's the deal with humans? My wife is human. I'm on my tenth human wife, you know what I mean? I marry them when they're twenty and they've got cute arses, and sixty years later, it's like I've married the Crypt Keeper."

The crowd groaned. The audience sat around small round tables, nursing drinks. Most looked human. A few people wore flouncy shirts with ruffled collars—a few even in Elizabethan ruffs and velvet suits. But without seeing their fangs or sniffing them up close, it was hard to get a handle on which were vamps and which were fang-hags.

I took another step inside, surveying the layout of the place. A curtain hung at the back of the pub, forming a sort of makeshift stage. Maybe I could stake this comedian arsehole behind it. The handy thing about killing vampires was that they didn't leave a body behind—just a discreet pile of ashes, easy to miss in the dark.

"My wife is crazy." He spoke into the mic, and the feedback pierced the air. "You know, she tries to eat all natural. No GMOs, no preservatives. Then she gets these fake tits and Botox. So it's all well and good for her to eat quinoa, but she's poisoning my dinner with chemicals, innit? I don't want to drink that shit. Disgusting."

I loved it when my victims made it easy for me to forego the guilt.

"What are you booing me for?" he yelled.

I had no idea where Ruadan was, except that he was probably watching me from a dark corner.

With my box of glasses, I stalked behind the curtain.

It smelled of old beer and piss back there, and there wasn't much room—just enough for a small card table, a folding chair, and a few saggy costumes hanging on a crooked clothing rack. A door stood open to a unisex loo.

I dropped my glasses on the table, listening to the comedian haranguing the crowd about his human wife's tits. I pulled the stake from my cleavage, ready for action. I slid it behind my back so he wouldn't notice it.

As the crowd fell silent again, the raven-haired vampire stepped behind the curtain. His gaze swept up and down my body, and he flicked his black hair out of his eyes.

He licked his fangs. "Hello there, darling. You look like a fine bit of crumpet. You all right?"

"I'm fantastic." I smiled at him, then whipped out the stake and rammed it into his heart before he could see what was coming. His eyes widened with shock, and then his body blackened and cracked.

He collapsed into a pile of ash, and it clouded the air a bit. I tried not to breathe it in, disturbed by the idea of inhaling vampire particles into my lungs. I coughed.

One down, fourteen to go. I kicked the pile under the table, then tucked the stake back into my cleavage.

That was easy.

From the stage, the emcee's voice boomed over the pub.

"And our next act, directly from New York City—the Big Apple—is Arianna, with the hot new trend of glass smashing!"

Before heading out to the stage, I grabbed one of the stained dresses on the clothes rack—some sort of a fairy costume with a tulle skirt. I ripped the bodice until I had a long strip of fabric, and I wrapped it around my knuckles.

I flicked my hair over my shoulder, plastering a smile on my face. It probably came off like something between "deranged children's TV presenter" and the rictus of a clown-obsessed serial killer before he slit your throat. I had no idea how to put on a show. At least, I didn't know how to put on a show devoid of blood and severed limbs.

Already, I could feel the crowd tensing, as if my presence alone were putting them on edge. I scanned the audience, trying to pick out the real vampires from their goth admirers. I noticed a few fangs, but most kept their mouths shut. A few clearly looked like performers: an elderly woman slumped near the front, dressed in a Little Bo Peep burlesque outfit, nursing a martini; a scarecrow with a bongo drum.

How to lure the vampires out of this crowd of humans...

A small stool stood on the makeshift stage, and I dropped my box of glasses onto it. Then, I leaned into the microphone. "Hello, London!" I said in my American accent, and feedback pierced my ears.

A heavy silence greeted me. Little Bo Peep snorted dismissively. All right, old woman. I'll show you how it's done.

I cleared my throat. "I'm here to…smash glasses."

I hadn't thought much about what this would entail, but I was trying to improvise.

I took a deep, shaky breath. *Gods below,* could I just go back to killing people already?

When I scanned the room again, I caught a glimpse of violet eyes burning from an alcove. No one seemed to notice Ruadan. When I'd first met him, I found it hard to focus on him at all, as if his entire body were a blur of magic. Now, he stood out to me like a beacon.

As Ruadan came into focus through the whorls of his dark magic, I caught a distinct curl of his lips. Was he *smiling?* I'd never seen him smile. It was almost enough to put me right off my glass-smashing routine.

I wrapped the fabric a little tighter around my knuckles, then lifted the first glass. I tossed it in the air, giving the throw a bit of dramatic spin. As gravity pulled the glass down again, I slammed my fist into it. Shards of glass rained around me. A few people in the audience screamed—men, I was pretty sure.

I grabbed the next glass—a wineglass—and tossed that. As it fell, I drove my fist into the stem. That one didn't smash quite as spectacularly in the air as the first one had, but it did shatter on the floor. The act was still living up to its name.

Still—clearly, the pint glasses were better. So for my next trick, I grabbed one of the pint glasses. Before I threw it into the air, I surveyed the room. A blur of movement tightened my stomach. It wasn't Ruadan—I could still see him lurking in one of the alcoves, though his body was now completely alert. That meant it was one of the other novices, already here and killing vamps. And I'd only slaughtered one, so far.

All the vampires' eyes were on me—the insane woman on the stage. I'd given the other novices the perfect distraction to kill while I was stuck up here.

Baleros's twentieth law of power: Bring your enemy to you.

I unwrapped the cloth from my knuckles, then tossed the next pint glass in the air. Bare-fisted, I punched through it, and glass shattered around me. A few people screamed again, but some also clapped, and I was starting to feel a bit proud of my show. More importantly, I had just a hint of blood on my knuckles, which meant the vampires would be homing in on my scent.

Once a vampire had his senses locked on someone's particular smell, he wanted to pursue it.

They wouldn't rush for me. No—vampires who lived among humans had learned to restrain their wildest impulses. A vampire scenting blood was sort of like a man hitting on a beautiful woman in a bar. Usually, they took turns, to have a go one at a time, instead of just all crowding around at once. They were competitive, but they had a sense of propriety about it. It was, after all, a seduction.

I lifted a wineglass, throwing it high in the air, and I smashed it perfectly this time. Glass rained around me, and a few shards cut into my skin.

The humans were cheering louder now, a few even

whooping. If I ever made it out of the Institute alive, I could have a glittering career ahead of me.

One more glass—twirling into the air, catching in the golden lights—and I shattered it with my fist.

The audience roared their approval.

Now, blood streaked over my fist, and I raised my hand, waving it at the crowd. Blood dripped onto the stage. "Thank you, London! That's all for tonight!"

My good mood was dampened by the sight of Maddan's red hair, slinking in the shadows. I'd recognize his stupid, lumbering gait anywhere. But despite his awkward movements, he moved silently, like he was supposed to. Cloaked by shadows, he staked a vamp.

Prince Knob-end of the Wanktonians was showing me up, and I had to act fast.

At least the vampires had my scent now, which meant they'd pursue me. Through the crowd's cheers, I heard the owner bark something about "cleaning up that fucking mess," but I ignored him, slinking back to the loo behind the curtain.

When the vamps approached me, I had to slay them before any of them realized I was fae. I didn't want them to catch on that I was a spell-slayer before I had the chance to stake them.

I stepped into the loo and closed the door, readying my stake. Then, I inched open the door to peek outside.

It was only a few seconds before the first vampire prowled behind the curtain. He was tall and lean, with blond hair, spectacles, and a hint of stubble. In his Batman T-shirt and jeans, he nearly looked human—apart from the glowing red veins in his pupils.

He sniffed the air, and I flung open the door. I leaned against the doorframe, cocking a hip—trying to look seductive, and no doubt failing. I held the stake behind my back with one hand. "Why, hello there, young man," I drawled in my American accent.

"Hi." He smiled, showing off his fangs. "I'm Mike. Your act was very impressive. Perhaps we could—"

BAM. I slammed my stake into his chest, and his eyes flew open with shock. His body blackened, then crumbled into ash on the floor.

I frowned down at the pile. I almost felt bad about Mike. He actually seemed kind of nice, but the Old Gods must have their sacrificial blood.

In any case, he was properly dead now. I kicked the ashy pile to the side of the doorframe, sort of mashing it into the stained rug so no one would notice it.

I stepped out of the loo, closing the door behind me.

It was another twenty seconds before the next vampire rounded the corner—he looked about twenty-five, much shorter than the last. He wore a fedora and a beaded necklace.

Once more, I held the stake behind my back. It was amazing how easily male vamps would ignore a stake behind your back if you showed off some cleavage and stuck out your boobs a bit.

Fedora narrowed his eyes. "What happened to the other bloke? I thought I saw someone come back here."

I nodded at the closed door. "I wouldn't let him drink from me. He's in there, crying into his Batman T-shirt."

Fedora smirked. "Of course he is. But vampires shouldn't ask for permission. That's not how we operate. That's why they call me the Tamer of Women. I'm a legend—"

A stake to his chest cut off the rest of his seduction pitch. His skin cracked, desiccating before my eyes as it turned to ash. I coughed in a bit of charred vamp.

Three down. Now I needed to move outside before they

started to realize the vamps weren't coming back from behind the curtain. If I could lure—

The sound of shrieking interrupted my thoughts.

"Spell-slayers!"

Oh, balls. We'd been discovered.

I peered around the corner, and my breath caught in my throat as I realized one of the other novices had cocked it up again.

How long until the vampires realized that I was one of the slayers, too?

I gripped my stake.

The scene was chaos—vampires attacking humans, flinging them against walls, snatching them by their shirt collars to sniff them. They were trying to hunt out the fae. Given my position in the pub, I'd have to fight my way through a mob of fae-hunting vampires to get out.

My heart raced, and I scanned the pub until my gaze landed on Ruadan. In a cloud of inky magic, his violet eyes burned bright. He beckoned me toward him, summoning me to leave the pub with him. But maybe this was my opportunity to make up for the time I'd lost while I'd been stuck smashing glasses on stage.

Baleros's twenty-second law of power: Chaos is the opportunity to remake the world into your vision.

CHAPTER 10

One of the other novices had already outed us, which meant we weren't in the shadows anymore. Might as well make the most of it, use this as my chance to prove the Old Gods really *did* favor me. Just like in the old arena, my ability to kill would give me leverage.

As I started into the fray, I felt a whoosh of magic by my side—cold power pulsing over my skin. Then, I felt the warmth of Ruadan's body behind me. He reached out, grabbing my arm that held the stake.

He leaned down, whispering, "We need to go before they turn on you." His piney, apple-tinged scent surrounded me. For a brief, insane moment I had an urge to lean back into the security of his powerful body. Something about my days alone in the prison had left me desperate for another person's touch.

Instead, I shook my head. If he thought I was afraid of a few vampires, he really didn't know me at all.

"I need to win this," I said. "I need to get out of the prison you're keeping Ciara and me in. Killing gives me leverage. That's just how it's always been."

I ripped my arm from his grip, elbowed him hard in the chest, and then leapt onto one of the tables. I was heading for a vampire who'd started punching a human woman in the face. I slammed my stake down hard through the vamp's back, piercing his heart. As he crumbled to ash, I yanked out the stake, ready for my next victim.

From below, a blonde female vamp pointed at me. She screamed, "Spell-slayer!"

She leapt high into the air, arms outstretched. I brought my stake up hard into her heart. She burst into a cloud of ash in the air, and I inhaled a puff of blackened vampire.

Now, three male vamps were prowling closer. Too many to stake at once. Still, I'd take them all out, one at a time. I jumped off the table. When the first vampire ran for me—a large male with a shaved head—I grabbed his arm, using his velocity to hurl him into one of his friends. The move sent both crashing to the floor, and I whirled to drive my stake into the third one's heart. I sucked in a bit more ash as he crumbled.

The remaining vampires in the pub moved in closer, and a familiar feeling arced through my limbs—the glorious battle fury of the arena. It was a cold, brutal sensation, but in a way, it felt like home.

I ducked and pivoted, fending them off with an avalanche of fists and elbows—the occasional kick to the face. Whenever the chance presented itself, I slammed my stake into a vampire's heart.

Even without the lumen stone, my speed picked up. Battle rage sharpened my senses. Dust and ash rained down around me. Forget performing—this is what I was made for.

My attacks stalled when a vampire surprised me by gripping me by the hair, yanking back my head. I bashed my elbow into his gut. He bent over, holding his stomach. I slammed my stake through his back.

From the corner of my vision, I glimpsed Melusine staking a vamp who was coming for me. We were working pretty well together.

But the attack had thrown me off, and another knocked me to the ground. He was pinning me, clamping down on my wrists, so I brought my knee up hard into his groin, loosening his grip. I grabbed him by the back of the hair, pulling him off me. He smelled of petrol.

As I did, I caught sight of something that sent a jolt of fear racing through my blood. On his wrist, he had a tattoo of a bundle of sticks—the fascia. It was Baleros's symbol. My body began shaking. I knew that symbol well. Baleros had once burnt it into my wrist as a brand.

"Who are you?" I shrieked.

"He's coming for you." The vampire grinned. "He burns for you."

My heart thumped against my ribs, my mind racing. The butterscotch candies in my prison cell, the strange blaze of fire when he'd died…Baleros was never going to be easy to kill. Was it possible that he was alive?

I slammed my fist into the vampire's face over and over, until blood poured from his nose and mouth. "Where is he?" I screamed. Fury ripped through my mind. I was losing it.

The vampire's head lolled. "Who?"

I sat on top of him, my knees pressing into his chest, and I punched him again. He reeked of petrol…

"Where is Baleros?" I hit him again. "Is he alive?" Maybe I needed to hold back a little, or he wouldn't be able to answer any of my questions. I was about to break his jaw.

"Can't say." He tried to punch me, but I grabbed his fist.

I twisted his arm until I heard the snap of bone. I twisted it some more until the vampire screamed.

My gaze flicked up, just long enough to determine that Melusine was managing to keep the other vampires at bay with her shadow-leaping and staking routine. That was handy, because I needed answers from this fucker.

Pressing my knees into his chest, I held the stake up higher in the air.

"Tell me where he is."

"No."

"I'm not going to kill you now. This will be much worse."

I slammed the stake into his shoulder, pinning his body to the floor. Without a direct hit to the heart, it would hurt like hells, but it wouldn't kill him. He screamed again, the sound of agony piercing the air.

It took me a moment to realize the vampire was holding a lighter in one hand. Then it took another second to connect the lighter to the scent of petrol burning my nostrils.

The vamp brought the lighter to his lapel, and his body burst into flames. I leapt off him with a yelp, the flames already licking at my bare legs. A few embers burned on my dress, and I smacked them out with my hand. Luckily, the fabric was still damp.

And that's how a vampire commits suicide.

When his body had decayed into an ashy pile, silence fell over the pub. All of the vampires had turned into piles of ash on the floor, and the humans had all fled.

Unfortunately, Maddan was still here.

He glared at me, his lip curled. "What *are* you, gutter fae? How do you kill the way you do? What sort of nightmarish demon is your other half?"

I shrugged, slipping the ashy stake back into my cleavage. I was trying to act casual, but my entire body was shaking from what I'd just seen. *Is Baleros alive?*

I crossed to Maddan, narrowing my eyes at him. "What am I? I don't know, but it seems like the Old Gods don't have a problem with it. Seems like they sort of favor me. I killed at least ten vamps here tonight. What about you?"

I was beginning to *really* get into this "favored by the Old Gods" situation.

"There is only one spot," said Melusine. "If you win every trial, what does that mean for us?"

Maddan dusted off his expensive top. "It will never happen. Grand Master Savus would never allow a thieving, rule-breaking, criminal gutter whore to become a Shadow Fae." He raised his hand, and that bright red magic flickered between his fingertips. "Savus will keep you in a filthy cage until it's time to bring down the axe on your neck, or exalt you in the Institute. But before he does, I want to find out what this animal really is. I want to be the one to interrogate you."

He stepped closer, and my stomach tightened at the sight of the red magic. That stuff had *really* hurt. Still, I didn't want to give him the satisfaction of seeing fear on my face, so I schooled my features to calm.

I crossed my arms. "Is it just me, or are you a little creepy about your obsession with me?"

A dark smile curled his lips. "Should I visit you in your hole again? I did so enjoy seeing you crouching in filth, at my feet. It's the way it should be." He took a step closer. "I liked hearing you moan when I hurled my bone-ripping magic at you…almost as much as I liked hearing you moan when I hit you with the lust magic. What would happen if I used both at once? It would be fun to find out."

Violet magic pulsed between the fingers on his other hand.

"Stop it, Maddan," said Melusine. Green magic glowed from her fingertips. "I know seventeen types of attack spells. Fire magic, disease spells, pestilence spells, which are totally different…"

I gritted my teeth, tuning her out as she listed several

types of disease. I glared at Maddan, who toyed with the glowing magic at his fingertips.

Ruadan had promised me the Grand Master would have my head if I killed him. And if I tried to escape, he'd send every Shadow Fae in the world after me. So what was I supposed to do? Just allow him to torture me?

I narrowed my eyes, mentally calculating the best ways to hurt him. Slam his head into the table, then into my knee. I'd kick him in the chest; he'd fall back. Then, I'd take my stake—

Maddan hurled his magic at me—both red and violet at the same time.

Magic slammed into me, and I felt as if my body were exploding. Pain shot through my limbs—but strangely enough, it felt pleasurable at the same time. Waves of ecstasy shot through my muscles. A strange, euphoric agony surged, until my entire body was trembling. I dropped my stake.

I was starting to get the feeling that Savus was keeping me in the Institute not because of the Old Gods, but simply because he had a sick desire to torment me.

When I lifted my eyes, I had the satisfaction of watching Melusine hurl her green magic at Maddan.

Before my very eyes, I stared as lesions began to open on his skin.

"Syphilis," Melusine declared with pride. "Brought to Europe in the fifteenth century by Columbus. Symptoms include: skin lesions, fever, hair loss, rotting skin…"

Maddan's screams drowned out the rest of her description.

Pain and euphoria still pulsed through me, racking my body. I had a hard time focusing on Maddan's torment.

The intense wave of dark magic over my skin told me that Ruadan was nearby.

"Novices." His voice was glacial. "We are done here."

He prowled under the flickering neon lights of the bar. His footfalls crunched over shattered glass, and his shadow magic snaked around him like ink through water. I didn't know when I'd get the chance, but I had to tell him about Baleros. I just couldn't do it in front of anyone else. Maybe—just maybe—Baleros was alive. And perhaps someone from the Institute had tipped him off about my location. My money was on Maddan, of course, but who the hells knew?

Ruadan was right. I couldn't trust anyone.

As the magic pulsed through my body, painful and sensual at the same time, I glanced at Ruadan.

I couldn't trust him either. But I was fairly certain he wanted Baleros to stay dead as much as I did.

CHAPTER 11

In Savus's throne room, I stood between Maddan and Melusine. With his silver arm, Savus gripped a skull-topped scepter.

My mind roiled with panicked thoughts about Baleros.

He's coming for you. He burns for you.

Ruadan stood behind us, his dark magic whispering over my body.

I cast a quick look at Maddan. Regrettably, the Institute's healers had already fixed his little syphilis issue. The lesions and rotting nose had already cleared up.

I had not been offered the benefit of healers, and no one here seemed to care if my body still burned from Maddan's magic. Half lust, half pain, and all distracting.

I felt acutely aware of Ruadan's presence just behind me, and some insane impulse had me wanting to back up into his body and press myself against him.

For one thing, the lust magic was still swooping through my core, heating my body. For another, I instinctively knew that Ruadan could heal the remnants of the pain eating at my bones and muscles. But I held my ground, and I clenched my fists to avoid letting Maddan catch on to how much he'd screwed with me.

I sucked in a deep breath.

He burns for you. What did it all mean?

On the throne before us, Savus's body glowed with pale, silver light.

"I asked you to kill within the shadows," he began, "and once again you failed. You slaughtered every vampire, true, but you terrified the humans at the same time. What is the explanation for this?"

From behind, Ruadan stepped forward, and I felt the power of his magic snaking up my spine. It licked at my body, taking away some of my pain.

"One of your novices got sloppy," said Ruadan, "staking a vampire in the open—just by the entrance. The other vampires saw the attack, and pandemonium erupted."

Savus lifted his eyebrow, glaring at me. "Which novice?"

"Prince Maddan."

I could see Savus's jaw visibly tighten, and he narrowed his eyes. That was not the answer he wanted. "Are you sure it was the prince?"

"Yes." A cold fury imbued that one little word. Ruadan didn't like being questioned.

Of course, if it weren't for the crown, *he* would be the alpha.

Grand Master Savus cocked his head. "Fine. Your novice did well enough, today. Bring her back to her cell."

I stepped forward, rage simmering in my chest. "I'm not doing that."

Savus's eyes flashed with fury, and wavering candlelight glinted off his silver crown. "You don't have a choice. Unless we decide that you are fit to become a knight, which is unlikely, you are our prisoner. It's the cell or your head on the execution block."

I looked down at my fingernails, feigning nonchalance. "You can't execute me. It's clear now that the Old Gods favor me. Once again, I killed more than the other novices. You keep trying to throw obstacles in my way, but it's not working. I have no lumen stone. I had no money. I was in a cell for days, getting hit with Maddan's bone-shattering magic. No proper food. And I *still* killed more vampires than they did. The Old Gods favor me, and you can't defy them. They're the ones who keep you on the throne."

Maddan's face reddened. "Perhaps they're just keeping the gutter whore alive as a joke?"

I crossed my arms, desperate to get out of here and to speak to Ruadan. There were a few holes burned into the fabric of my dress from the would-be-assassin's explosion. The vampire was a deranged psycho, but gods-damn, that man was committed. He'd gone out on his terms. He'd committed to his task—abduct me, or die trying.

I was going out on my own terms, too, even if it meant self-destructing.

I cocked a hip, the pleasant smile still warming my features. "If I have to stay in that prison, perhaps I'll sit out the next trial. And the next one. I simply won't participate. That's not what the Old Gods want, is it?"

"What if I simply kill you?" he hissed.

I shrugged. "Then kill me." I was calling his bluff. If he killed me, he'd lose that precious silver crown of his, and anyone would be able to overthrow him.

His jaw tightened. "Perhaps you don't value your life. If that's not a deterrent, how about I torture you?"

"You're already letting Maddan torture me in the prison. I don't see how it could get worse. Maybe you should have kept a leash on him if you wanted better leverage."

Savus's low growl reverberated through my gut. "What do you want?"

"I just want what the other novices have. A lumen stone. A proper room for Ciara and me to sleep in. Oh, and some of that amazing fae food. That's all I ask for. What every other novice has."

Grand Master Savus cut a sharp look at Ruadan. "Bring her to the Liorcan Tower. She may sleep in one of the servants' rooms. Her human will remain in a separate room. And please understand that our guards will be watching you at all times." He snarled. "No lumen stone. This is as far as I'm willing to bend before I rip your body to pieces."

Well, it was better than the devil's arsecrack, I supposed.

* * *

THROUGH AN ARCHED STONE HALLWAY, I walked by Ruadan's side. Candlelight danced over the hall, gilding his perfect features. He towered over me, casting me in his shadow.

Two guards trailed behind us, prepared to listen to anything we might say.

I couldn't quite explain the deep sense of betrayal I felt whenever I looked at him. After all—I'd betrayed *him.* I'd stabbed him, and run off with his precious lumen stone. But then we'd worked together to take down Baleros, and for some idiotic reason, I'd hoped it had meant something. I'd hoped for forgiveness.

A pit opened in the hollow of my stomach. He'd done a few nice things for me in the past—blankets, healing. Letting me keep the lumen stone. Allowing me to live. A pathetic part of me had desperately wanted to believe that he'd done those things because he'd cared.

Now that I'd returned to the Institute, I realized how stupid that was. He'd killed his last two novices. He'd lured me back here, only to throw me in a prison. He called me "gutter fae" instead of using my name. He'd left me to rot in the Palatial Room, healing me just enough so that I didn't die. He wanted me punished as much as Savus did.

My jaw tightened. When did I start giving a shit if anyone called me "gutter fae"? This wasn't like me. Something about him just got under my skin and drove me crazy.

Ruadan paused at a door, and it opened into a tiny room. This wasn't like the other rooms I'd seen. It was more like the size of a closet, with a single bed in the center. A plain, red rug lay on the stone floor near the bed.

I had no bath in here. Still, an archway opened into a tiny bathroom, so that was a step up from sleeping in my own filth.

I crossed into the bathroom, irritated to find that it was basically just a hole in the stone, with a bowl of water next to it for handwashing.

I breathed in deeply. The bedroom itself contained only two objects—the bed and the rug.

One of the guards—a broad-shouldered man with a long, aquiline nose and golden hair—crossed into the room. It took me a moment to recognize him, but he was the same guard I'd briefly charmed the last time I was at the Institute. He was the drunk one who'd nicknamed me *Viscountess von Tittington.* Creepy, but oddly endearing, and at least he didn't hate me.

Ruadan gestured at him. "Ealdun here will be your guard. He will remain in the room with you."

I stared at them. "In the room with me?"

Ealdun lifted his chin. "Grand Master Savus's orders." I noticed he wasn't calling me *Viscountess von Tittington* in front of Ruadan. In fact, he was making every effort not to look at me.

I shrugged. "Fine. Suit yourself. I hope you enjoy my singing, Ealdun, because I do love Taylor Swift."

"Enjoy the gutter fae," said Ruadan. He turned, stalking out the door in a blur of dark shadows.

I bit down hard on the urge to scream at him that he was a snobby twat. Truthfully, my heart tugged at his parting shot. I shoved my disappointment deep down inside, willing myself to forget about it.

I'd already known what he was like. I'd told myself that trusting him was a mistake—that he'd lead me to the execution block, and the betrayal would kill me before the blade ever did. I'd been right.

CHAPTER 12

Fatigue pulsed through my body, and the cold stone floor was calling to me. When I wasn't sleeping in a festering dung hole, I slept on a stone floor.

I began singing—off key—as I pulled off my boots.

I took a little pleasure at the grimace on Ealdun's face as I sang. I had nothing to change into, so I curled up on the floor, still wearing my black dress. It was covered in rainwater, vampire ash, and my own blood. I *really* wanted a bath.

I was on the other side of the bed from Ealdun, shielded from his view on the stone floor. Maddan's magic still flickered through my veins—hot and cold, pleasure and pain, and the intensity overwhelmed me. I felt as if my body were clenching and unclenching, racing with sensations. My nipples chafed against the filthy fabric of my dress.

Even so, my eyes floated shut, and I tried to calm myself with thoughts of tree-dappled hills—just like the ones I'd dreamt about in the cell.

I didn't even notice as I drifted off to sleep.

I awoke to the scent of pine, and a warm hand on my

back. Violet eyes pierced the darkness. A heavy rain hammered the windows outside. For just a moment, I wanted to wrap my arms around Ruadan, to let his warmth and his magic soothe me.

Then, rage and that sense of betrayal welled in my chest as I stared up at him. Humiliatingly, tears pricked my eyes, and I fought the urge to punch him in his beautiful face.

"How did you get in here?" I whispered.

He brushed his hand over my waist, pulling the remaining bone-shattering magic from my body. I sighed with relief, closing my eyes again for a moment.

Then, I met his gaze again. "Have you come to call me a gutter fae again?" As soon as the words were out of my mouth, I regretted them. I'd just let him know that his words had gotten to me, when I'd been trying to pretend that I didn't care.

Baleros's first law of power: Knowledge gives you control.

"Don't raise your voice too high," he whispered. He nodded at the other side of the room.

I peered over the bed, where I found Ealdun slumped on the floor, sleeping.

"What happened to him?" I asked in a whisper.

"I made him fall asleep. The same thing I've done to Maddan every night to keep him away from your cell."

"You've been putting Maddan to sleep? Why?"

Ruadan raised his perfect eyebrows. "Because I didn't want him to torture you anymore."

I took a deep breath. More confusion. "Why are you here?"

"I saw the vampire immolate himself. What happened?"

I sucked in a deep, shaky breath. "On his wrist, I caught a glimpse of Baleros's tattoo. He said, 'he's coming for you.' And 'he burns for you.' He works for Baleros. Not to mention the fact that…" I paused, not wanting to explain the whole butterscotch thing. "Someone was screwing with me when I was in the Palatial Room, tossing me little symbols of my relationship with Baleros. Is there any chance that monster could still be alive?"

Shadows flitted through Ruadan's eyes. "I can't entirely explain why his body ignited after I killed him. But I did kill him. Are you sure it was Baleros's symbol?"

I lifted the sleeve of my dress, showing him the brutal scar on the underside of my wrist. "Oh, I'd know his symbol anywhere. I had the same mark on my skin. Except, because I was a gladiator, it was a brand instead of a tattoo."

A powerful pulse of Ruadan's dark magic thrummed over my skin, and shadows pooled in his eyes. It seemed the topic of Baleros provoked some kind of primal rage in Ruadan.

"What happened to yours?"

"I cut it off, obviously. I didn't want to live with his brand."

"Why not?"

I gritted my teeth. "*Why not?* Are you insane? Because he's a monster who made me think I was a monster. I didn't want him to control me any more than he already does. I mean, any more than he did. I've always wanted him dead. What the hells do you think?" I willed my heartbeat to slow, realizing that I'd lost control of my emotions.

Ruadan's icy magic slid over my skin. "You say you wanted him dead, and yet you did his bidding, and you allowed him to live in the arena." Anger flickered in his violet eyes, and the ice had returned to his voice.

"Why do you hate him so much? Because he turned on the Shadow Fae?"

A sharp breath. "Something like that."

I could tell by the hesitation in his response that it wasn't the full answer. Moreover, I'd turned on the Institute of the Shadow Fae, and he hadn't killed me.

Whatever the case, Ruadan was hiding important things from me. He trusted me no more than I trusted him.

CHAPTER 13

"You haven't explained to me why you failed to kill him. I brought the darkness, like you asked." A ripple of dark magic thrummed over my skin. "But you didn't even try. Why?"

Knowledge gives you power over a person. How much power did I want Ruadan to have? I supposed he already knew I cared about Ciara, considering I'd insisted on bringing her here. He could already use her as leverage if he wanted.

"He took Ciara," I said. "He was holding her in a cage, and he was going to kill her. I didn't kill Baleros in the arena because I was there to save Ciara, and in the moment, I could only do one or the other. I didn't have an iron weapon, and I needed answers from him. As soon as I knew where she was, I went after her."

Silver glinted in his eyes, and his magic stroked the back of my neck. "You stabbed me to protect Ciara."

"Yes. I still think *stabbed* is a bit much. It didn't kill you. It was more like a...you know, like a setback, I'd call it."

"You setbacked me in the chest, with a knife," he said, with a straight face.

I almost wondered if that was a joke, but Melusine had warned me that the fae nobility were incapable of joking.

"Did you consider using iron?" he asked.

Only the rain filled the silence, until I added, "Let's not dwell on what might have been. I'm alive. You're alive. Let's move forward."

He cocked his head, studying me closely. I had the impression he was reconsidering something.

He reached for me, lifting my wrist, and he traced his fingertips over the scarred skin where I'd cut off Baleros's brand. The feel of his fingertips on my skin sent an unwelcome rush of tingles through my body. I had a hard time reconciling this gentle touch with the Ruadan who called me gutter fae and dragged me over stones.

"You hate Baleros." His intonation suggested this was some sort of revelation.

"Of course I hate him. He's been messing with my head since I was fourteen."

Shadows slid through Ruadan's eyes, and his fingers tensed on my skin. "That's how old you were when he enslaved you?"

"Yes."

I realized he was still holding my wrist, still tracing the scarred skin. Why did that scar fascinate him so much? Whatever the case, the feel of his gentle fingertips over such a vulnerable part of my body made my cheeks warm.

Gods-damned incubi.

"And you think Baleros could still be alive? That he sent an assassin after you?" He was leaning in closer, his velvety voice, now sensual, slipping around my skin like a caress.

What was with this guy? Were his hot and cold moods just another method of control?

I stared at the hypnotic swirl of his fingers over my skin. Somehow, I knew the truth deep within my bones. Baleros would never be easy to kill. "I think he's alive. I think he's working with someone from the Institute, someone who tried to screw with my mind in prison. Someone who tipped him off about the trial tonight. Obviously, my money is on Maddan, because he's one of the worst living creatures on Earth. But the vampire lit himself on fire before I got the chance to torture him for information, so that's just a guess."

Ruadan was gently pulling me closer by my wrist—the gesture almost protective. "You've got a guard in the room with you, and more outside the door. In theory, you're safe. But Baleros has sent his spies into the Institute before. It's not entirely outside the realm of possibility that some of the guards could be working for him."

"He's sent spies here? Into the Institute?"

"The last two novices I executed."

My eyes widened. "Oh." Slowly, understanding was beginning to dawn in my mind. "That's why you killed them."

"When I first saw you fight Aengus, I knew that Baleros had trained you. I considered killing you. Then, I thought maybe you would lead me to him."

I swallowed hard. "I get it. You thought I was a drunk, undisciplined gutter fae slob, but you still wanted me here to lead you to Baleros."

"Once I learned you'd been a gladiator, it changed things a little. Not the slob part, I still think that's true. But I understood you were not a spy. You were a slave."

My cheeks flushed. "Not a fan of that term."

"Baleros had ways of controlling his gladiators through mental torment. I started to think maybe you'd turn against him if given the chance. In the arena, you nearly did. Until you let him live."

"Is that why you've been..." I gestured into the air, unwilling to finish my sentence. There was no way in hells I was letting him know he'd *hurt my feelings.*

"What?"

It was embarrassing how much I'd wanted it all to be an act, and it really had nothing to do with anything. We had a common goal: kill Baleros. That was it. Were those *tears* stinging my eyes? Mortifying.

I turned away from him. *Caring about people is a liability.* "Never mind. You can fuck off now. You interrupted my sleep. And don't come back into my room without my permission. I don't need your unwelcome intrusions. Do you understand?"

He dropped my wrist, and my entire body suddenly felt cold.

I waited until I felt the whoosh of his shadowy magic over my skin.

When I turned back, Ruadan was gone. A pit opened in my chest, and I shivered. I lay back down on the cold stone floor and closed my eyes. But this time, dreams of Emain didn't enter my mind.

Instead, an old memory rose in my skull—one I'd long tried to forget. A field, rotten with fae bodies...

My eyes snapped open again, and I stared at the ceiling. Maybe I'd just stay awake tonight.

With Ruadan gone, I realized he'd left something behind for me—my bug-out bag. This time, there was no way it was an accident. He'd actually gone into the prison to fetch it for me.

Was he being *nice*?

I crushed the dangerous thought as soon as it entered my mind.

CHAPTER 14

Ealdun poured me another measure of whiskey. I needed the drink, considering I'd been stuck in this tiny room for the past twenty-four hours. While the other novices had been training, I'd been locked in here with no one for company but my guard. Worse, he'd alternated with a much more unpleasant guard who tried to insist that I call him "Master."

I supposed it was part of my ongoing punishment, but I had no bath in here, and no clothes to change into. I was still wearing the ashy, blood-stained dress from the last trial, and I'd just stopped wearing underwear all together. I did my best to wash with the little bowl of water, while Ealdun repeatedly asked if he could help.

Unlike *Master,* Ealdun loved to chat. After one day, I knew that he never wanted to have children, that he liked thongs on a woman but women didn't wear them enough these days, and that he had nightmares about being smothered by mermaids' breasts—and also longed for such a death.

He wasn't the *worst* guard in the world, given that we had similar hobbies. Namely, whiskey and vulgarity.

Still, none of this was helping me get ready for the next trial. In fact, all the sitting around and drinking was basically the opposite of training for combat.

"I'm not sure I'm going to survive my next trial, Ealdun."

"Nonsense. Whiskey will fortify you. It's fortifying me. I've got a bit of a cold." Ealdun sniffed. "Whiskey's good for a cold."

I frowned. "Is it?"

He nodded. "Kills the bug, innit. Gets the bug drunk, and the bug dies of all the alcohol." He knocked back his shot. "They can't process alcohol, right? Bugs don't have the right sort of livers for it."

Ealdun really wasn't the brightest bulb, but I just nodded rather than arguing.

"My dog Scroton has a bit of whiskey every morning."

I stared at him. "First of all, you have a dog named Scroton? Please tell me that's an Ancient Fae word."

"It is, actually."

"What does it mean?"

He sipped his drink. "Scrotum."

"Right." Despite all the alcohol, tension gripped my entire body. As much as I enjoyed sitting around and drinking whiskey with idiots, a cloud of doom was hanging over me. I had to pass the next trial, or I faced a certain and excruciating death at the hands of Savus, or perhaps Ruadan. And what would happen to Ciara if I died? I wouldn't be here to protect her. I *had* to exploit every advantage I could.

So I poured Ealdun another shot. The man had a tolerance to rival Hannibal's elephants, and we were now on day two of my attempt to get him completely wankered.

I had a powerful buzz going on, but I'd only been drinking one shot for every three of his. Any more alcohol and I'd be unable to do anything.

I filled his glass to the top. "Best get that bug nice and drunk so he doesn't do any damage."

Ealdun mumbled under his breath, and he took another sip. He was muttering something about how there were two kinds of women: those who took it up the bum, and those who did not, but I did my best to ignore his binary classification of the entire female gender.

When his head lolled, his eyes closed, and I knew I had my chance to sneak out of there.

Baleros's seventeenth law of power: Never let an opportunity go to waste.

I wanted to find Ruadan to learn what I could for my next trial. Ever since I'd told him, "Fuck off and don't come back in my room," I'd regretted it a bit. Yes, I'd been angry at him. He'd hurt my feelings, and I didn't want to let him do it again.

But this was bigger than hurt feelings. This was my survival. And whether or not I liked it, my life—and Ciara's—depended on Ruadan's help.

When Ealdun's snores began to echo off the stones, I crouched down on the floor.

It hadn't taken long for me to find the way that Ruadan had entered the room. After my temper had cooled, I'd simply lifted the rug.

He was the Wraith, yes, but he couldn't transport himself through material things like walls and windows. He'd actually just walked into the room—albeit in his silent and stealthy Wraith-like way.

While Ealdun snored, I pulled up the rug. Inset into the stone, lay a wooden trapdoor. I'd found it during the night, but I hadn't been able to risk lifting it without Ealdun noticing.

The trapdoor creaked, revealing a ladder that led down

one level into darkness. A quick glance at Ealdun told me he was still asleep.

I jammed my hand into my bug-out bag, and pulled out my headlamp. I flicked it on. After drying out, the trusty thing was working again.

With the light beaming from my head, I slipped into the hole, climbing down the ladder in my bare feet.

The dank tunnel air whispered over my bare thighs. At the bottom of the ladder, my feet hit wet, slimy rock. The white circle of light from my head illuminated glistening stone walls. Here, the air hung heavy with the smell of moss and mildew, and maybe a bit of fungus. I regretted not having slipped my boots on, but I'd been too tipsy to think of it.

Down here in the tunnel, I could feel myself stumbling. The combination of whiskey and the sludge on the floor made it hard to balance.

Still, I was starting to home in on the scent I'd been trying to track. Pine, a hint of apples. For whatever reason, Ruadan's smell now stood out to me among all the others.

Locked iron grates interrupted the ceiling in some places, and light pierced the cracks, flecking the stone floor.

At last, the scent of pine and apples grew more powerful, and I knew I was drawing closer to him. But when the sound of footfalls began echoing off the walls, my heart slammed against my ribs. I flicked off my headlamp, my muscles tensing. I wasn't alone down here. Who in the seven hells was that? I had nothing to use as a weapon, so I hoped I could take them with my bare hands.

Time for a quick retreat.

I whirled, breaking into a run on the slick floor. I nearly slipped a few times, but I righted myself. I hadn't gotten very far when a rush of cold magic slid over my skin—then, a powerful arm hooked around my waist.

When he pulled me closer, I slowed down long enough to breathe in the scent of pine. Ruadan's powerful arms enveloped me, and I felt strangely vulnerable in his grasp.

I willed my heartbeat to slow. "Ruadan. Fancy meeting you here."

I flicked my headlamp back on.

"Arianna. I was hoping you'd come for me." He was still holding on tight to me, his grip confusing me with its warmth and protectiveness. "I was just on my way to see you." His deep voice stroked my skin.

"Even after I forbade you from intruding?"

"Yes. Whether or not the intrusion is unwelcome, you need me to survive your next trial."

"Right. Well, that's why I came to find you, as it happens."

Ruadan loosened his grip on me, and he turned back in the other direction. "You reek of whiskey."

"That's not all I reek of. I'm hoping to take a bath in your room."

His thrilling magic snaked over my body.

Ruadan shook his head. "Savus can't know that I'm helping you."

"Why?"

Shadows lashed the air around him, sucking up all the light from my headlamp.

"The Grand Master must think that I hate you," Ruadan explained. "If he believes I favor you, he'll continue to find worse and worse ways to torment you."

I frowned. "I don't understand."

Ruadan shook his head. "He hates me, and he wants to crush anything and anyone that I might…favor. That's why I couldn't heal you fully—Maddan had to think you were still injured. It's why I've had to create a spectacle of derision for you. I need Savus to believe that it's real."

"Why does he hate you?"

His jaw tightened, and a heavy silence filled the room. For a moment, I was certain Ruadan had lapsed into his characteristic "vow of silence" trick, until he finally answered. "Grand Master Savus and I have a history. That's all."

That illuminated almost nothing, but what did I expect? It was Ruadan, after all.

I narrowed my eyes at him. "When you dragged me down the corridor and threw me in the Palatial Room, did you leave the backpack with me on purpose?"

"I rarely make mistakes."

"And when you called me 'gutter fae'—"

"It's important that the others think I'm disdainful of you, or things will become much worse for you."

I loosed a breath I'd been holding. Hearing that his cruelty had all been for show felt like a weight off my shoulders, and I hated that I cared so much.

"It'll be fine if I take a bath and change. I'll convince Ealdun that he got me the clothes I asked for. He won't remember a thing from tonight."

We reached a trapdoor, and Ruadan paused. He pushed on it, and it slammed open into his room. Then, he leaned down and grabbed me by the waist. He hoisted me up into the light.

My head was definitely swimming from the booze, and I toppled over a little, onto the stone floor. By the time Ruadan pulled himself inside, I'd managed to right myself, straightening my hair like I was totally composed.

Ruadan closed the door behind him. "You bypassed Ealdun."

"He drinks a lot. He's snoring over the table right now."

"That's why I chose him as your guard. He's terrible at his job. And as you might have guessed, I chose your room strategically."

"I don't suppose you have a change of clothes that would fit me?"

Ruadan crossed his arms, his body growing still. "You really risked coming here just for a bath?"

"No, I also want to learn about my next trial. I'd very much like to avoid that whole iron pincers situation."

His electrifying magic kissed my skin. "The next task will be difficult for you."

Great. "Fill me in while I'm bathing."

I'm not sure at which point I'd decided that I liked being naked around Ruadan—possibly it had been when I'd been in his bed, hepped-up on lust magic, and I'd felt the way his body had tensed. Then, there was the bath where his body had again become rigid with tension.

As far as I could tell, he lived to brood, and I liked ruining it for him.

So as I started across to the bathroom, I tugged up the hem of my dress, making sure he got a view of my bum. He might be a stronger fighter than I was, but his pent-up desire gave me some power over him, and I could practically *feel* his gaze drinking in my body as I pulled off the dress.

Completely naked, I let my hips sway a little as I crossed into the bathroom, and Ruadan's magic whispered over my skin, raising the hair on my nape. Ice frosted the air as a pulse of his magic billowed through the room, and my nipples hardened. A smile curled my lips.

I was *definitely* getting to him.

Once through the arched doorway, I tossed the dress on the floor next to the tub, which was already burbling with spring-fed warm water. Steam rose from the surface. I stepped into the hot bath, the water reddening my legs.

I slipped all the way in, closing my eyes. I didn't really want to have to leave here and listen to Ealdun's snoring all night, but I suppose I'd have to.

"Are you coming in?" I asked.

"While you bathe?" The torches in the room flickered on and off.

Ruadan crossed into the room, his movements as predatory as ever, and he refused to look at me. Then, his dark magic snaked through the air. It curled around the torch flames until it snuffed all the light from the room. With his entrance, he'd smothered every light particle.

I let out a long sigh. "Now I don't know where the soap is. You'll have to come over and help me."

"You're trying to tempt me. Is it just me, or do you thrive in chaos?"

"Chaos is an opportunity. Don't you know that? Anyway, I don't know what the problem is—oh that's right. The whole virginity thing. No wonder you get angry so easily."

"For the love of the gods." Irritation laced his voice. "I'm not a virgin. I've only been here fifteen years."

"Right. Just celibate. And why is it that you have to be celibate?"

"Grand Master Savus's orders."

"He's an arsehole."

"He believes self-denial encourages mental fortitude. Incidentally, that brings us to the next trial. You will need mental fortitude."

It was unfortunate that he couldn't see my eye roll in the dark. "I thought you said I'd be bad at it. I'm perfectly mentally strong."

"You lack discipline. You showed up drunk tonight, and within minutes you were also naked."

"I mean, yes..." The bath felt amazing, and I clumsily felt around the stone rim of the tub until my hand slid over the bar of soap. "Naked and drunk. I can see why that would look bad on paper. In my defense, I have had a hell of a week."

"You solve most of your problems with violence. You were unable to withstand the gorta without slaughtering him. You stabbed—sorry—stopped my heart with a silver setback in my aorta."

Spring water burbled into the tub, pooling between my thighs. "Are we just pointing out each other's flaws now? Because as far as I can tell, you're a giant killjoy with no friends."

"You surround yourself by those weaker than you, because they can't control you, and you use them to distract you from things you'd rather forget."

I gritted my teeth, now furiously scrubbing at my arms with the soap. "Look, criticize it all you want, but I *did* pass the gorta trial." I inhaled deeply, willing my body to relax in the warm spring water. "So what is this trial, another hunger fae?"

"No. It's called a gwyllion. A female fae who came to London from Snowdonia. You will be asked to fetch something from her lair. And when you do, she will torment you with your worst fears and memories. Your mission will be to withstand the mental torture for as long as it lasts. You cannot run from her."

For once, I was quiet, soaping my body in silence. Unfortunately, Ruadan was right. I would not be good at that. This was not like killing vampires, and I did not welcome the idea of a Welsh mountain fae rooting around in my mind.

CHAPTER 15

"How do I prepare for it?" I asked, after a moment.

"The same way you prepare for anything," he said. "You practice."

Even in the warmth of the bath, my body was tensing. There were many things I'd rather not think about. I ran the soap over my legs, scrubbing harder, wearing the damn bar down to a nub. Still, I would show Ruadan that I had plenty of mental fortitude. "How?"

"I can help you summon your darkest memories."

"You can?"

"I'm a demigod of darkness."

"Oh, right." I splashed water over my shoulders, dreading what was to come. "Is that Ancient Fae for 'brooding killjoy with no friends'? Sounds like the same idea."

"Get out of the bath."

"You're very bossy, you know that?" Still, I complied with his orders, and I stood.

Water dripped down my naked body, and I squeezed out my hair into the tub. I hadn't planned ahead with a towel or anything like that, so my wet feet slapped against the stone floor. Maybe it was the whiskey, but I felt an overwhelming urge to move closer to Ruadan. Barefoot, I crossed over to him until I was standing right next to his heat. Warmth radiated off his body onto my damp skin. I inched just a little closer, until my breasts brushed against his chest.

His magic rushed off him in a wave of power, flowing over my skin. Then—for just a moment—his fingers were on my waist. Instantly, my back arched.

I couldn't see him in the dark, but I looked up at him anyway.

With a low growl, he snatched his hand away. "Get dressed." His voice was curt, commanding.

A smile curled my lips. And because I was me, I inched just a little closer, pressing my body against his. His muscles completely tensed, and it was like standing pressed up against a stone wall. "But I don't have any clothes," I protested.

He pulled away from me, stalking out of the bathroom, taking his darkness with him. The shadows snapped back into his body as he prowled to his dresser. I stared at him from behind, frowning at his arms. He was wearing a black T-shirt, and red scars slashed across the back of his powerful biceps.

"What happened to your arms?" It must have been iron—the only substance he wouldn't heal from easily.

He didn't answer. Instead, he pulled open the drawer of his bureau.

"Someone attacked you with iron," I said. "How did they manage to get that close?"

He selected a black shirt from his drawer and held it out without looking at me.

Whatever had happened to him, I felt bad about it, so I'd stop tormenting him with my boobs for now. I crossed to him, grabbing the shirt from his hand, and I pulled it over my head. It reached about midway down my thighs. My wet hair dampened the shoulders. "Thanks. You can be helpful sometimes. When you're not locking me in dung holes and whatnot."

"We have work to do." He turned to me, silver glinting in his eyes. "Sit down. On the floor."

I did as instructed, planting my bottom on the cold flagstones. I hugged myself. Ruadan's room always felt a little colder than the rest of the Institute. That was his magic, I guess.

I gazed up at him. "I am at a disadvantage for this task. I think I have more terrible memories than most."

"You'll get through it."

I sucked in a deep breath. I didn't want to do this, but I wanted to prove to him that I could. Maybe I lacked discipline, but I wanted to impress Ruadan.

His magic began darkening the room, curling around the flickering candles and snaking over the rays of moonlight that beamed in from the windows. The shadows pulsed in and out, like the breath of a living thing.

Already, a pit was opening in my chest, and coldness seeped into my blood. I shivered, my teeth chattering. Ruadan's power washed over me, and my blood pounded in my ears.

I closed my eyes, listening to the sound of my own heartbeat. Then, darkness slammed into me, burying me alive. My heart raced, and I felt like I was suffocating, as if I needed to claw at the dirt above my head. I gasped, a gnawing void widening in my chest. Ruadan was killing me.

Then, light pierced the darkness—sun rays filtering through oak leaves, my heart pattering like a frightened rabbit. Oh gods, not this…

I wasn't really there. I needed to remember, this was just a memory. It wasn't real. Not anymore.

I was running barefoot over the mossy forest soil, my feet crunching on twigs. They'd come for us—the invaders from another land. He'd told me to run, but I couldn't just leave them there. I had to go back. Sweat dampened my skin, and my heart was racing out of control. I turned, heading back in the other direction. I pumped my arms hard, my breath coming in short, sharp gasps. Panic raked its claws through my heart. But the smell of blood, of death was growing stronger, filling my nostrils. I knew what I was about to find there. I didn't want to see it.

Anger rose in me. Why did I have to remember this? Why was Ruadan forcing me to relive this?

When I breached the clearing, horror slammed me in the chest. There, staining the fields in red, a legion of dead fae soldiers, fed the earth with their blood…

An ache built in my chest, cutting me so sharply I thought I might die. I had to stop this.

Fury erupted, and I lashed out with violence, my knuckles hitting flesh, striking and striking—

The illusion fell away from me as Ruadan caught my wrists.

My body was trembling, my legs ready to give way. My knuckles ached like I'd been punching walls. Ruadan stared down at me, his cold gaze slicing right through me. He didn't say a word, but he didn't need to. I knew what he was thinking—something along the lines of "you lack discipline."

I ripped my hands from his grasp and gritted my teeth. "Let's go again."

"Sit down." That irritating, commanding tone.

My body trembled as I took a seat on the floor again.

My chest was heaving, nostrils flared. Ruadan was only trying to prepare me, but right now, I wanted to setback Grand Master Savus right in the face. I could kill things.

Assassins were supposed to kill things. So why did I need to revisit the horrible things from my past?

Once more, Ruadan's magic breathed darkness into the room, and the shadows slowly pulsed—in and out, in and out, the movement slow and hypnotic. I needed him to know that he was wrong, that I was perfectly disciplined. I was capable of controlling myself.

The air around me cooled, until my breath misted in front of my face. Then, the blanket of darkness smothered me, burying me underground. Panic surged, and I gasped for breath. A cool tongue of shadowy magic licked up my spine. My lungs felt heavy, the darkness all-encompassing.

Then, fire flashed before my eyes. A yawning void had opened within my chest, eating at me from the inside out. The arena's torches cast wavering light over the empty stone seats, the red dirt. There was no audience. A dark power vibrated through my body, trembling along my bones, and the sound of the ocean roared in my ears.

No audience. No, today Baleros had wanted me to train. It had been an experiment, really. What would happen if he set fourteen opponents against me? If there were enough people to fight me, could I be taken down?

I felt weightless, unmoored from the earth, as if I were floating in space. Now falling. Death coiled around me.

Horror slid through my gut as I stared down at what I'd done. Fourteen opponents lay dead at my feet, their skin turning black. Blood trickled from their mouths, their ears. I knew one of them, a fire demon named Elish. Baleros had kept him in a cage not far from mine. Once, when I'd been starving after a week in the metal box, he'd tried to pass over his bowl of gruel to me. It had tipped over in the dirt, but I hadn't forgotten the attempt.

I screamed within my own mind, the sound curling

around the inside of my skull until I couldn't hear my own thoughts anymore.

I wouldn't have killed Elish if I could have helped it. But this was a power I couldn't control.

Sometimes I didn't mind killing, but this—this controlled me. Darkness had pooled in my mind, and then nothing but death.

All the breath had left my lungs.

A slow clap filled the arena, and Baleros crossed over the dirt.

"Arianna. I knew you were special, but I never imagined you possessed this level of evil. Now do you understand why you must be kept in a cage? Why a monster like you must be controlled?"

My fingers twitched, rage surging sharp and hot until it burned away the illusion. And there it was again—that terrible feeling of power trembling up my bones, the sound of the ocean roaring in my ears. A wild, uncontrollable force of destruction, threatening to break free.

Ruadan was standing there, staring down at me in his billowing cloud of shadow magic. Tendrils of magic snaked over his stupidly beautiful face. So calm, so controlled, his gaze was pure ice. Gritting my teeth, I willed my heartbeat to slow again. I needed to stay in control.

I rose on unsteady feet, and I crossed to Ruadan. Maybe he could see I was about to lose it, because he grabbed onto me, pulling me in close, and his soothing magic began stroking my skin, warming me. My breathing slowed, my heartbeat calmed as he pulled me in tight against him. He ran a hand down the back of my hair, soothing me, and his piney scent wrapped around me. For a moment, I almost had the urge to rest my head against his chest, to close my eyes.

Then, he leaned down and whispered in my ear. "What are you?"

I froze. I couldn't let him know.

I pulled away from him, staring at his face. "We're done now." My voice was so cold I nearly didn't recognize it. "You don't know what you're playing with. Don't come to my room again."

He didn't say a thing as I pulled up the wooden trapdoor in the floor. I dropped down into the darkness, my footfalls echoing.

I hurried away from him as fast as I could. Maybe he was right. Maybe I lacked discipline. For some reason, the thought of disappointing him made my chest clench. But the truth was, Ruadan had no idea what would happen if he pushed my limits too far, and I didn't need any more terrible memories to haunt my worst nightmares.

CHAPTER 16

Ealdun lay slumped over the table, his snores echoing off the stone walls. If it weren't for the line of guards stationed outside my room, I'd be able to escape.

Tonight, as requested, Ealdun had brought me a piece of paper and a pencil. I'd told him I needed it to play tic-tac-toe to kill the boredom.

Oddly enough, I'd started to think of him as a friend. He'd actually been a perfect gentleman, and he'd been delighted to have an audience for his interminable Scroton stories.

Ealdun's snores rang out as I crossed to the secret trapdoor. I pulled it up, and slid my legs into the hole, jumping down. I hit the damp stone floor with a soft thud.

After a few nights in my little room, I'd convinced Ealdun to fetch me some clothes. I now wore a pair of black leggings and a dark shirt. Much more respectable than the T-shirt and bare arse I'd been sporting for a few days.

This time in the tunnel, I wasn't heading for Ruadan, but for Ciara's room. I wasn't sure exactly where to find it, but I tuned into her smell—wildflowers and a bit of musk.

If I told the Shadow Fae that I wanted Ciara released, I'd

be giving the game away. They'd guess my next move—that I was planning an escape to avoid my execution, and I wanted my friend out of here. I couldn't telegraph my actions that way. Instead, she needed to escape while I was *at* the trial, before they knew what was coming.

As I walked, I traced my fingertips over the damp wall.

Despite my warnings that he needed to leave me alone, Ruadan had returned one night after another. He'd slipped into the room while I slept, put my guard to sleep, then tried to convince me to practice my mental discipline skills. I kept telling him *no.*

I knew I was proving him right, that I was only demonstrating my lack of discipline, and a flash of fury lit me up. Still, I couldn't let myself completely lose control.

I understood that I had to face the gwyllion, and that it would be unpleasant. But the fact was, if Ruadan pushed me too far, he might end up dead. I wasn't willing to risk it.

Still, I didn't get much sleep those nights. My mind churned, over and over. If I failed this task, the Shadow Fae would kill me. Would Ruadan do it? I didn't want to kill him, but would he bring the blade down onto my throat? Would he demonstrate his mental fortitude by forcing himself to kill someone he liked? Assuming he even liked me at all. I really didn't know. Whatever the case, the thought of dying at Ruadan's hands never failed to send a sharp pang of sadness tearing through my chest.

Already, I'd explored the entire passageway. Unfortunately, the tunnels didn't offer any escape. Mossy stone walls bookended either side of the tunnel. Besides the door into my room, the only other door opened into Ruadan's room. Still, I could find a way to get a message to Ciara before we both busted out of here.

I traced my fingertips over the scar on my wrist. Once the Shadow Fae purges had closed down the arena, I'd cut

Baleros's brand off the inside of my wrist. Ciara had been there to help me patch it up. She'd treated it with a human ointment called Bacitracin that I'd never seen before, then she'd patched it up with cotton bandages. It had healed a lot better than the wounds she'd treated below ground.

I breathed in the damp air. I liked it down here in the dank tunnels, and at least I didn't have Ruadan trying to torment me with brutal visions from my past. The tunnel seemed to go on forever, an immense labyrinth that wended through the castle.

It took about ten minutes before Ciara's particular smell grew stronger. I frowned when I reached her room. There was no trapdoor and no way for me to enter, but a metal grate was inset into the stone. I thought it might be the bathroom.

If I failed the trial, I'd go on the run again, straight away. I'd evade Ruadan for the rest of my life.

But what did that mean for Ciara? She'd be trapped here in the Institute. The Shadow Fae would use her as leverage.

And that meant I had to get her out of here now.

Below the locked grate to her room, I pulled out my pencil and paper, scribbling on it.

Ciara. I may have to go on the run after the next trial. You will need to leave here. I will find you in...

I chewed my lip, trying to think of a location. *Oxford. Near the University. Stay there until I find you. And destroy this message.*

Could I really escape Ruadan at all, even if I wanted to? I had a feeling his tracking skills were unparalleled.

I pushed my worries to the back of my skull and gently tapped the grate.

After a moment, Ciara's face appeared, her dark eyes wide. Without a word, I slid the paper through an opening in the grate.

She read it, then nodded at me. She disappeared for a second, then reappeared, scribbling something of her own. She thrust the piece of paper through the hole.

You can't run from them. Ruadan will find you.

Right. Ruadan was the devil. The devil wore many faces. I'd heard this before. But she didn't know my real fear—if I let them prod at the worst things in my mind, I might not be able to control who I killed.

I scribbled on the paper. *It may be our only option. I'll try to disguise my scent if I have to escape.*

My chest tightened at the thought of Ruadan hunting me down, an iron sword in his hand. I couldn't allow him to find me.

The betrayal would kill me before the blade ever did.

More furious scribbling from Ciara.

I don't trust any fae except you. When we get out of here, we will celebrate with corn dogs, sloppy joes, and snow cones. I want to bathe in the blood of our enemies and fashion their skulls into battle drums. Are you with me?

I blinked at her message, beginning to think I was not the scarier friend in our pair.

Yes. I wrote back. *Skulls and corn dogs. Sounds like a good time. I have to go. Get ready to escape.*

I shoved the note through the grate, then turned, crossing back down the passage. Now, I needed to convince Ealdun to help me. All he had to do was incapacitate Ciara's guard, and she could sneak through a window into the darkness.

When I reached the light that pooled into the tunnel from my room, I leapt into the air, catching the edge of the opening. I hoisted myself up, and scrambled into the room. Quietly, I closed the trap door, then covered it with the rug.

Ealdun still slept on the table, his head partially propped up on his hand. A thin stream of drool trickled out of the corner of his mouth.

"Ealdun," I said quietly.

He snorted, his eyes still closed.

"Ealdun," I said a little louder.

He murmured something about nipples, still asleep.

"Ealdun!" I shouted, and I smacked the hand propping up his head.

He jolted awake, looking dazed for a moment and blinking in the light. His gormless expression almost had me feeling bad for hitting him.

"You fell asleep," I said.

He scowled at me. "I did not. I was meditating, innit."

"Right. Look, I won't tell anyone. But while we're on the topic of doing each other favors, I have a favor to ask of you."

"If you want me to free you, you can forget it right now. Savus scares the ever-loving shit out of me. And Ruadan is even worse. I'm not letting you loose on the world."

"Ealdun. We're friends, right?"

"I suppose so."

"I'd never ask you to risk your life like that. But I would ask you to maybe…find a way to distract or incapacitate Ciara's guard. She's only a human. And she's only here because I wanted her here. It's time for her to leave."

He frowned at me. "I don't know if this is a good idea."

"No one will blame you. They'll blame the guard who failed."

He scratched his cheek. "I never liked Drem, but…"

I let out a long sigh. "Look, if you help me, I know where you can find a mermaid in Cornwall. I will give you specific directions. She's often drunk on cider and she's not very picky. She's perfect for you."

He scratched his cheek, eyebrows raising. "A mermaid?"

"Yep. Huge rack."

"Sold. What do I need to do?"

"Just, you know, distract Drem until Ciara can get out the window and go off to the human world where she belongs."

Ealdun's eyes were just starting to drift closed again, when a knock sounded in the room. My body tensed.

Gods below. I'd made it back just in time for another trial.

Ealdun frowned at me. "Expecting someone?"

"Nope, but it's not as though anyone ever fills me in."

"Who is it?" Ealdun shouted.

"Ruadan." His voice permeated the door. "I'm here to collect the gutter fae prisoner."

I clenched my jaw. So we were back to that, were we?

I stared at Ealdun. "Will you do what I asked? Please?"

He rubbed his eyes. "I'll distract Drem. That's all I'm promising. His fault if she leaves, right?"

"Exactly."

Ealdun stood, then pulled open the door. Ruadan stood in the hallway wearing his cloak. Shadows slashed the air around him.

I crossed to the door, unwilling to meet Ruadan's gaze. I didn't need to see the disapproval there, after a week of me refusing to train with him.

We both knew the truth. I had no mental discipline.

"It's time for your next trial."

Ruddy afternoon sunlight streamed in through the ancient windowpanes in the hall. Like a living thing, Ruadan's magic did its best to smother it.

A shiver of dread snaked up my spine. "I'm ready," I lied.

But I wasn't moving. I stood in the doorway, a weight pressing on my chest.

I needed to make a run for it tonight, but I wasn't sure I could escape the Wraith if my life depended on it.

And the truth was, my life did depend on it.

CHAPTER 17

I clutched my bug-out bag, stalking along the pavement at dusk. The neon lights of a tattoo parlor flickered over a puddle.

For tonight's trial, Maddan had decided to wear a golden crown, since he had basically no idea how to appear normal in public. Like me, Melusine wore simple black clothes, tightly fitted. At least Maddan seemed to be ignoring me this evening.

Our mentors walked behind us as we trod the rain-slicked street in East London. Rain dampened my hair and clothes, but a few sun rays pierced the clouds. The sun was just beginning to set, casting lurid nectarine light over Brick Lane and staining the rain clouds with purple.

Even in the rain, a few people stood smoking outside some of the pubs and nightclubs, the collars of their coats pulled up high.

I turned, glancing back at Ruadan. Menace curled off him, and as we walked, humans scrambled out of the way.

Aengus walked with his hands in his pockets, his green eyes scanning everything around him.

Then, he narrowed his eyes at me. "Will you be stabbing any of us tonight, Arianna?"

"Keep talking, and I might," I muttered.

Maddan's mentor, a knight named Cronan, skulked behind him, his black hair falling in his eyes. He was giving me a death stare, too. Ever since my escape from the Institute, I wasn't the most popular person among the Shadow Fae.

I loosed a sigh, focusing on the street ahead of me. A mustached man in flannel stumbled out of a chicken shop, dropping the chicken bone in his hand when he caught a glimpse of Ruadan's eerie eyes and his enormous frame.

Nothing to see here, folks. Just a group of creepy-ass fae, stalking the streets on a Thursday night—one of us wearing a crown.

I hadn't expected to find a mountain fae in the center of East London's nightlife, but stranger things had happened. If I had to make a fast escape, I was lucky there were plenty of people around to mask my scent.

"Turn left," said Aengus.

We hurried across Commercial Street onto a narrow lane. A multistory car park rose up to our right, its white metal fences giving it the appearance of a skeleton.

"This place reeks of humans," said Maddan. "What are we doing here?"

Aengus paused in front of the white barriers of the car park. As he did, its appearance began to shift. Now, a brick wall shimmered into view where the barriers had been.

A glamoured building in the center of East London.

As the glamour further thinned, a black storefront came into view. The setting sun pierced the shop's colored glass windows. Through the muddy hues of orange and purple, I could see a shop crammed with strange knick-knacks: stuffed hummingbirds in bell jars, an antelope's skull, a gaping-eyed doll with a red-lipped grin who was probably stealing my soul.

The gold lettering over the shop window read *Bronwen's.*

A gust of wind swept over the street, toying with a set of wind chimes. Honestly, I really preferred the vampires to this creepy place. When I glanced toward the main road, I saw a bleached-blond woman in a white dress wander toward the entrance to our street. Then, her brow furrowed as if she was confused, she pivoted, then walked away.

It seemed some sort of glamour stopped humans from walking down this street, as if they simply didn't see it.

I felt a tap on my shoulder, and I turned to see Melusine. She wore her blue hair in a messy bun on her head. "Yeah, I'm not too worried about this one. We go inside, she gets in our heads. We just stand there. What's the problem? I've had mental torture before. You know, one of my broom friends used to call me a loser. All the time. Just this high-pitched voice, shrieking at me. Sounded like my voice in a weird way."

Aengus stepped forward, tapping her arm. "This would be a good time to clear your thoughts, Melusine."

She ignored him. "Anyway, the point is, I have three ways of maintaining mental discipline. I take baths with small chunks of ice, I hold my breath as long as I can, and I also take baths with large chunks of ice."

"Very impressive." Was the test of mental torture starting early, or…?

"Maddan has a lot of mental fortitude, too," she went on. "Not because he's strong, but because has no feelings."

I frowned. "Shit. That's actually a really good point."

"No feelings means no fear, right? I put two and two together. Now *you* have feelings. A lot of rage. Some fear. Some sadness. Mostly rage. I'm not so sure how this will go for you. I think you might crack."

You and me both. "Thanks for the vote of confidence."

She shrugged. "I tell it like I see it."

The clacking of boots on pavement caught my attention, and I turned to see Grand Master Savus stalking toward us, his silver arm glinting in the ruddy light. Mist curled around him, forming shapes as it moved—a snarling wolf, a writhing snake.

As he glared at me, he bared his canines. But when I looked at his crown, my chest began to warm. It looked *withered,* the silvery spindles wilting. It had lost its luster, turned now into a dull gray.

A smile curled my lips. The Old Gods were turning against him.

But *why?* Why in the seven hells would he risk all that power just to get me out of here? It didn't make sense. I understood he wanted Maddan because he came from a rich family, and I was just a gutter fae. But there had to be more to it than that.

Savus stopped in front of the colored glass windows, his crown sagging on his head.

"Novices," he said. "Tonight, you must withstand Bronwen's torment for as long as she delivers it. This is a test of discipline, of mental fortitude. Most of all, it requires that you are able to face yourself." His icy gaze fell on Melusine. "Melusine, you're first. Enter the shop. Endure the torment for as long as the gwyllion delivers it. You may not run away from her. Return with a deck of tarot cards. Hand them back to me."

She nodded, her expression resolute. The door chimed as she pulled it open. She slipped into the gloomy shop, the door creaking closed behind her.

I shifted on the darkening street. I had no idea what mental torture Melusine would be facing, but I was sure it had to do with her sad birthday parties—the ones where she tried to force her brooms to eat cake. Or, maybe something much darker lurked in her past.

After a few minutes, a keening noise wound through the streets, piercing me to the core. It took me a moment to recognize it as Melusine's voice, and a shudder danced up my spine.

Sounded a lot worse than a sad birthday.

Maddan stepped in front of me, smiling to show off his canines. He looked like he was about to start something. And why wouldn't he? Nothing could touch him. I wasn't supposed to kill him. Ruadan couldn't help me, or the Shadow Fae might think he cared for me. And as we all knew, caring about someone put them at risk.

A chill slithered over my skin as Maddan skulked around me, now standing behind my back. When he brushed my hair off my shoulder, I shuddered. While Melusine's screams continued to pierce the air, I closed my eyes, envisioning how I would kill Maddan someday. I wondered if I could punch right through the center of his chest and rip out his heart. If I did, would he live long enough to watch me throw it at him? That would be special.

His hand gripped my waist, and he leaned down. "What will the gwyllion stir up in your mind, gutter fae? The days you spent roaming the streets, desperately fucking—"

His sentence was cut off, and I whirled to see Ruadan lifting him in the air. With a ferocious snarl, the Wraith hurled Maddan at a parked car across the street. Maddan's body dented the car.

Then, Ruadan's cold, shadowy gaze slid to Grand Master Savus.

When I was a kid—back when I lived in the woods—I once watched two stags fighting for supremacy. A younger one and an older one, antlers locked, until the younger gored the old stag, piercing his neck with his horns.

Ruadan's glare promised savagery, his magic lashing the air around him.

Tension rippled across the horizon, until at last Savus's crown began to slip, and he pushed it back up on his head.

He cleared his throat. "Get up, Maddan," was all he said.

The Old Gods were turning against Grand Master Savus. Had Ruadan just upended the hierarchy of the entire Institute?

I crossed my arms, a smile warming my face. "Are we allowed to beat Maddan now? This day is turning out better than I'd anticipated."

But already, my mood was darkening. The Old Gods might be turning against Grand Master Savus, but for now, he still held the power. If I failed this task, my life was still in his hands.

Maddan was cradling his arm, his face red. "My father is the king of Elfame," he said. "Do you know how much money he has given to the Institute?"

Before anyone had the chance to answer, Melusine slammed through the door, her face pale. Then, she collapsed into a heap on the pavement in front of the shop, her teeth chattering.

Gods below. A gnawing void opened in my chest.

"A failure," bellowed Grand Master Savus, nudging the crown up further on his head. "Her time with us is done. Aengus, take her away from here."

My stomach sank. At least she didn't face the threat of execution for a failure, as I did. She'd just be sent back to the broom people who hated her.

Savus lifted his silver arm, beckoning Maddan closer to the door. "Prince Maddan. Enter, please. Return to us with a golden apple."

Maddan sneered at Melusine's heaped form on the ground, then stepped over her and into the darkened shop.

CHAPTER 18

Aengus crossed to Melusine, helping her up. Her entire body was shaking.

I inhaled deeply, listening for the sounds of Maddan's tormented screams.

Silence.

It was just as Melusine had said. Psychopaths didn't feel things. Maddan felt no guilt, no emotional pain. He was ruled only by a stark sense of self-preservation. The prince of Elfame was as empty as that creepy doll's vacant stare.

Just a few moments later, Maddan stepped out of the shop, gripping a gleaming apple in his hand.

Smiling, he tossed it in the air and caught it again. "I thought this task was supposed to be hard."

"Congratulations." I shot him a fake smile. "You have no soul. You must be so proud."

He handed the apple to Savus, then smirked at me. "Have fun."

"Arianna," Savus barked. "Go. Return with the gwyllion's teeth. Endure the torment in the shop for as long as she delivers it."

I sputtered. "Her *teeth?*"

"That's what I said." His tone suggested this was the most reasonable request in the world.

I narrowed my eyes at him. "Right. That's perfectly sensible. I'll pull out all her teeth and deliver them to you." Seven hells.

Still, that was my assignment, and I'd try to complete it.

I pulled open the door, and its chimes made me shiver.

Inside, thin rays of light streamed through the colored glass, illuminating rows of dolls and corked vials of colored powders and potions. Shelves towered over me on either side, and the warped wooden floor creaked under my feet.

A porcelain doll stared at me, half her head shorn, her mouth blood-red. She wore a dingy petticoat. I shivered at the sight of her. And when her jaw opened, my heart skipped a beat. She started to scream, and I clamped my hands over my ears. Bizarrely, it sounded like my own voice.

When her scream died down, I started moving deeper into the shop. From the ceiling, sagging teddy bears hung from hooks.

At the rear of the shop stood a woman in a green tracksuit, her back to me. Lavender hair—the same shade as mine—tumbled over her shoulders, and she had a cute figure. But when she turned to face me, my heart skipped a beat.

Amber eyes—the same shade as mine—stared out of a gaunt, haggard face.

I swallowed hard. How did one politely ask for a person's teeth?

"I need your teeth." Not like that, I was sure. "Let me rephrase that. Um, I must have the teeth from your head." Nope, that wasn't it either.

My fists clenched. I couldn't just attack her and yank her teeth out. She seemed like a harmless elderly woman, and I had some moral code. Plus, I was supposed to endure the mental torture first.

She grinned at me, displaying her long rows of teeth, and the hair on the back of my neck stood on end.

"Sorry, I'm not good with people," I went on. "I lived in a cage…" The rest of my sentence died out. Why was I telling her this? I had no idea what I was doing here.

My gaze flicked to the iron hooks hanging from the ceiling. *Good for killing.* No. No. I was not supposed to kill her.

My pulse started racing, and a cold sweat rose on my brow. "It's not important. Just, underground cage—"

A wall of black slammed into me, darkening my mind, and I fell to the ground, my knees hammering the wood. Darkness smothered me, spilling into my lungs like ink.

Then, a flash of light. I was running through the forest, barefoot. My heart was a hunted rabbit, and I knew what was coming. I didn't want to see it.

When I reached the edge of the wood, my blood roared in my ears.

It wasn't just the bodies of fae soldiers littering the ground. Not just the invaders.

My mother lay there, too, blood dripping from her mouth, a thin red line down her beautiful skin.

I have to get out of here. I have to run…

I turned, rushing for the portal as fast as I could. I'd leave home forever.

The image shifted. Hunger rippled through my stomach, and I rolled to the side, fingers in the dirt. After a week in the iron box, I was too weak to stand. Dirt was under my nails, in the cracks of the dried skin on my hands. It was in my mouth, my nostrils. It got everywhere.

Baleros stood over me. "My little monster. I think a week in the box did you good. Taught you your place. Creatures like you need to be controlled. You look like a sweet thing, but things aren't always what they seem. Do you understand?"

My mouth had gone completely dry. He hadn't given me enough water in the box. The hunger cut through me so deeply it didn't even feel like hunger anymore. It felt like a living thing eating me from the inside out. As I lay on the dirt, my legs shook. How much torment could an immortal body take?

"But you must be starving," said Baleros. "I brought my little monster a present."

He tossed the butterscotch sweet into the dirt of my cage. Starving, trembling. My fingers scrambling in the dirt. I grasped the butterscotch, then clutched it to my chest.

Another wave of darkness pulled me under, and my mind flickered with the image of my mother, my screams piercing the air.

He killed her…

This wasn't real. It was just a memory. Gods below, I had to stop this.

All the air had left my lungs, and I was drowning in the memory.

My dirty fingers, desperately grasping for the sweet...

What sort of creature would do this to a person? What sort of malevolent being would force you to relive the worst moments of your life? A fae that fed off pain. A fae that should die.

The vision disappeared before my eyes, and I was back in the shop, staring into the gwyllion's aged face. She grinned, showing off her long teeth. "Baleros is coming for you. He's going to make you his again. He's going to make you crawl in the dirt for your little sweeties. Arianna. What a joke that is. That's not your real name, is it?" She was shrieking now, and

I clamped my hands over my ears. "Not your real name! Things aren't always what they seem. Baleros knows that. Is that the real reason you want him dead? To keep your little secret? To keep him from telling people what a monster you really are?"

Blackness descended, claiming my mind. A hot flash of violence erupted in my brain, that familiar brutality that always lurked under the depths.

"Not your real name!" Her voice rang in my ears like a death knell. "Things aren't always what they seem."

I gasped, my vision clearing once more. I blinked at the iron hook in my hand. Blood dripped from the tip, and my stomach turned.

Then, slowly, my heartbeat slowed. My breathing slowed. I let the clear air fill my lungs.

When the haze of rage dissipated from my mind, I stared down at what I'd done.

The gwyllion lay on the floor. My throat tightened. It seemed that while she was tormenting me with my memories, I'd ripped one of the iron hooks from the ceiling, and I'd rammed it into her throat. Her blood had sprayed all over a collection of Victorian dolls. Apparently, I'd also smashed her mouth with the hook, because her broken teeth now lay on the floor next to her body. The gwyllion stared up at the ceiling, wide-eyed. Her hair was no longer purple, her eyes no longer amber. Both had shifted to a dull gray.

High-pitched screaming pierced my ears. "Not your real name! What a monster you really are!"

It took me a little while to realize it was that gods-damned creepy doll, shrieking in my own voice.

Oh, seven hells. I was supposed to withstand the mental torture for as long as she delivered it, and I'd killed her instead.

With a shaking hand, I grabbed her shattered teeth. I stared at them in my palm. Then, I stuffed them in my pocket. I didn't suppose the teeth alone would get me out of this situation.

The doll's screams had shifted to an accusation. "Killed her! Killed her!"

I looked down at my blood-soaked clothes. I'd done exactly what I *wasn't* supposed to do. I'd completely screwed up the task.

My heart began to slam against my ribs, and I scanned the shop's back wall, desperate for an exit. It was time to go on the run, wasn't it?

The doll's shrieks had died down.

Jars of preserved body parts stood on a table before a grubby window, and I grimaced at the sight of them.

I glanced back at the door. A silhouette loomed through the glass. It had gone too quiet in here. Was someone about to come in?

I rushed back to the screaming doll, lifting it by the torso. I felt a porcelain skeleton under its dress. The creepy thing blinked at me.

"Scream," I said.

The doll blinked again.

I let the darkness pool in me, the rage, the destruction. "Scream," I said again, my voice laced with cold fury.

The doll opened its red mouth and unleashed a shriek, a mimic of my own terror. I dropped it back on its shelf. Right now, I was just glad I'd had the foresight to get Ciara out of the Institute.

Adrenaline surged in my blood, and I could only hope that Ciara was already on her way to Oxford.

I climbed over the table, careful not to break any jars. Then I slid open the window, and it creaked up. At last, I'd pulled it open high enough to slip through. It opened onto a narrow London street, on the opposite side of the building from the other Shadow Fae. Night had fallen, giving me a little cover of darkness.

I'd found myself once again on the run, heading for one of London's rivers.

CHAPTER 19

My sodden clothing dampened the seat in the narrow canal boat. I glanced up at the stars, breathing in the clear air as I steered the boat. In the dark, I cracked open another Budweiser—not my favorite beer, but it would have to do. I hadn't found any food in the boat, so the calories from the beer would have to fill me.

Rivers made it hard to track a person. While the creepy doll had screamed into the shop, mimicking my voice, I'd had just enough time to escape before the Shadow Fae noticed anything amiss. I'd run south to the Thames. Then, I'd let the river carry me east until I reached the River Lea.

From there, I'd swum north against the current, until I reached an abandoned canal boat.

Now, I was sitting in someone's boat, drinking their beer. I shoved my hand into my bug-out bag, desperate for food, but found only a few crumbs of sugar. I pulled out my head-lamp and flicked it on. I needed to snatch a few hours of sleep.

Someone would likely report the boat stolen, which

meant I'd have to abandon it, but it was working for me for now.

I knocked back the rest of my beer, then slowed the propeller as I reached a stony mooring point. Using the tiller, I slowly steered it in.

I had no idea where I was, but I'd been moving north of London for a few hours. Oak and maple trees lined the canal.

With the boat safely moored, I stepped off into the soft grass, my body aching from my long swim through the rivers. My muscles burned.

My wet clothes clung to my body. I lay down beneath an oak tree, and I closed my eyes. As sleep overtook me, I found myself walking through an apple grove, dressed in nothing but a short, silky dress—cream-colored. Moonlight silvered the leaves and fruit around me. A man stood at the other end of the orchard, dressed in a black cloak. I couldn't see his face, but his dark magic whipped the air around him, and violet eyes pierced the darkness. My skin began heating, breasts peaking under my silk dress. I could imagine how his hands would feel cupping between my legs.

As I crossed to him, my pulse raced, and I pulled off the dress…

* * *

When I awoke, a wave of horror slammed into me. I was no longer in the park. Somehow—while I'd been sleeping—I'd returned to the Palatial Room. The rough stones bit into my back, and my bones ached.

What in the seven hells?

A layer of grime covered every inch of my skin and my damp, black clothing. How in the gods' names had I ended up *here*? I wanted to scream, but screaming would do me no good.

A guard stood directly across from me, chewing tobacco. He spat onto the sludgy ground. It was the guard who'd threatened to cut our tits off. The one I wanted to punch in the dick.

At this point, all I really knew was that it had not been a successful escape.

I swallowed hard, my mouth dry. When a shadow loomed over the cell, my heart sank. Ruadan's violet eyes burned in the gloom.

"Arianna."

"You threw me in the dung hole again," I snarled. "How did this even happen?"

"You ran. Did you really think you could outrun me?"

"Did you really think I wouldn't try? I'm facing my execution here."

He slid a key into the lock, and the door creaked open. "Come with me."

My legs were shaking as I stood, my stomach turning in flips. "Where are we going?"

"We're going to face Grand Master Savus. He believes you should die."

I clenched my teeth. It was just as I'd thought—the betrayal felt like a death blow. "You dragged me back here just to kill me. You could have just let me go," I hissed. "What difference would it make to you?"

As we walked up the stairs, he slid his gaze to me. "The Old Gods don't want you to die."

"But I failed the task. I thought I had to keep winning in order to demonstrate the approval of the Old Gods."

"Did you fail?"

I frowned as we moved up the stairs. "I slammed a hook into the gwyllion's throat while she was feasting on my worst memories."

We reached a metal gate at the top of the stairs, and Ruadan unlocked it. It swung open into a vaulted corridor.

"I noticed that," he said. "She is quite dead."

I had no idea what he was talking about. All I knew was that my heart was racing. Despite Ruadan's assurances, I felt as if I were on my way to my own execution.

My mind was flailing out of control, blood roaring. "How did I even end up here? I don't remember anything after I fell asleep under the tree. How did you find me? I traveled in the rivers."

"Your dreams."

"My dreams," I repeated. He had an amazing knack for answering things in a way that elucidated nothing.

"I can see them in my mind, and hear them. They vibrate, like a song, each with their own signature. If I tune into your dreams, they beckon me."

I'm not sure what horrified me more—the fact that he could track me so easily, or the fact that he might have witnessed my sex dream starring him. If I remembered correctly, we'd gotten to know each other really well up against the trunk of an apple tree.

"When you say you can see my dreams—"

"The orchard, yes." He kept his gaze straight ahead.

My cheeks burned. "That's very intrusive, do you know that? You shouldn't spy on people's dreams."

"It was a beautiful dream."

I snarled, my face heating. Suddenly, I'd forgotten about my possibly impending death. "That's not the point. The point is that it was mine. You shouldn't pry."

It wasn't until I realized that we'd entered Grand Master Savus's hall that I focused again.

On his throne of rock, Savus loomed over us. His crown looked even more withered, now a dark gray. The other mentors stood in the hall—along with Maddan. As the only remaining novice, he beamed with pride. His golden crown gleamed on his head. And here I was, literally covered in filth from the dung hole.

But Maddan wasn't the worst of my problems. A low, rocky slab rested on the floor by my feet. It took me a moment to recognize what it was—an execution block. At the sight of it, my hand began to twitch, and an icy chill licked up my spine.

Death is coming.

My heart beat like a war drum. I felt as if I were falling, my body becoming weightless. I felt unmoored, dropping through space. An icy wind gusted through my hair.

Savus nodded at one of his guards, who held an iron sword in the air. The guard crossed to Ruadan, who gripped the sword by the jeweled hilt. The world felt unsteady beneath my feet.

Would he execute me here?

Deep inside, I felt myself plummeting. My fingers twitched again, and a song of death sang in my veins. A yawning void opened within my chest, and a phantom wind tore at my hair. Weightless.

It's happening again. Death is coming.

They didn't know what I really was, that I'd be the one person to make it out of here alive.

"Kneel," Savus commanded. "You couldn't live with dignity, but perhaps you can die with it. Rest your neck on the block."

I wouldn't kneel for him again. I would kill him. My cold gaze slid to Maddan, who was staring at me expectantly, waiting to witness my death. In a few moments, he'd be lying on the floor, bleeding from the mouth.

I no longer felt as if I were on the earth at all, and I slid my gaze to Ruadan. "You betrayed me." My voice didn't quite sound like my own, and it scared even me.

But Ruadan's eyes weren't on me. No, he was still staring straight ahead, looking at Savus. Icy wind surged through my veins. I was plummeting in a void. Did they realize they were all about to die? It didn't seem that way.

"I don't know what you're giving me the sword for," said Ruadan. His voice was calm, subduing. "She completed the task, just as she was supposed to. Clearly, the Old Gods continue to favor her."

That was all it took to feel that I was back on the earth. The whisper of death left my mind, my feet meeting the stone floor with a lurch.

But what the hells was he talking about?

Ruadan looked at me, his powerful magic pulsing off his body. "You have the teeth, don't you, Arianna?"

I shoved my hand into my damn pocket, feeling the jagged, broken teeth. I'd nearly forgotten about them. "I do."

I pulled them out, showing them to Savus. My hand was shaking so hard I could barely keep them in my palm.

But as I held them out, the cogs in my mind began to turn. Maybe I *had* done what Savus had asked.

Endure the mental torment in the shop for as long as she delivers it.

Savus steepled his fingers, staring at Ruadan. "She slaughtered the gwyllion."

"She endured the mental torment for as long as the creature delivered it. She did exactly what was asked. She ceased enduring the torment when the gwyllion ceased to deliver it."

Savus now gripped the edge of his throne. His silver crown began to slide from his head, and he pushed it back up again. He gritted his teeth, his face paling. "That was not what I meant and you know it."

Ruadan's magic iced the room. "Look at your crown, Grand Master Savus. You know in your heart what the Old Gods want."

"Control her. Whip her. Beat her into obedience. Whatever it takes. Or you will no longer be welcome here at the Institute, Ruadan."

Ruadan straightened. He didn't answer, but his dark magic whipped at the air around him like a hurricane of shadows.

Maddan's face had gone bright red. When he turned to look at me, he held out his hands in a grip suggesting he was going to choke me to death. I'd welcome the chance to fight him hand-to-hand.

Maddan had no idea how close he had come to losing his life, just moments before. Death was a power I couldn't control, but I was starting to think it rose within me when I thought I was about to die.

Ruadan turned to walk out of the hall. I faintly heard the words on his lips as he leaned down to whisper to me, "You're staying with me, now."

CHAPTER 20

I sat at the stone table in Ruadan's room, dressed in one of his black shirts. Since Savus's crown had begun to wither, something had shifted between him and Savus. A change in the balance of power. But how long would that last?

I took another bite of the steak in front of me, the texture so soft it seemed to melt in my mouth. I leaned back in the chair, closing my eyes as I ate it. Gods, it tasted amazing.

As I finished the steak, a question burned in my mind, and I had to ask it. "Grand Master Savus's crown is literally wilting before our eyes. Could another Shadow Fae usurp his powers?"

"Without the approval of the Old Gods, we are no longer beholden to a magical hierarchy. Physically, I could kill him now. But there is another force keeping him in power, and the Shadow Fae High Council would not tolerate such an assassination. They would send knights from all across the world to dispatch the usurper."

I swirled the wine in my glass. "Even if the Old Gods strip him of his power?"

"We would need proof of wrongdoing. A crime, a betrayal of some sort. A semblance of a trial."

"You told me that you have a history with Grand Master Savus. You said that Savus would want to crush anyone that you might favor just to get to you. That's why you were dragging me over the stones and calling me a gutter fae." It was a classic Baleros move—use others to get to your real target.

"That's right."

"Considering that your 'favor' resulted in bruises on my arse and far too much time in the Palatial Room, I think maybe you could shed a little light on that history."

A long silence stretched between us, heavy as wet soil.

Darkness consumed the light around him. "He is my mother's cousin. Fifteen years ago, she was killed. Savus blames me for failing to protect her. He loathes me."

The weight of his words pressed on my chest. "He blames you for your mother's death? That must be incredibly painful. Has he really said that to you?"

"In his own way."

"What an arsehole," I snapped, anger roiling. I wanted to snap Savus's little neck. After a few moments, I asked, "What happened to your mother?"

No response, just a flash of silver in his eyes. So…he didn't want to talk about it. Fair enough—I more than understood the desire to keep the past hidden. "Never mind. Neither of us want to dwell on the torment of our personal histories. We have that in common. Best to keep the nightmares locked in their cages." The wine tasted delicious, and I let the berry flavors roll over my tongue. "Incidentally, that's what Baleros used to say about me."

Ruadan had gone still as the stone walls. "You have a nightmarish side. You thrive in chaos."

"Well, haven't you heard? According to Baleros, chaos is an opportunity to remake the world the way you want it." I arched an eyebrow at him, my mind flickering with the memory of that execution block. Ruadan had no idea how close he'd been to death. "There's something I'm missing. Why is Grand Master Savus so eager to kill me that he's willing to let his crown and his power wither? It can't just be the convenience of having a fae prince among the Shadow Fae."

"You're right, and I don't know. His behavior is irrational. He's driven by a strange compulsion to hurt you and perhaps kill you."

I frowned. "When you captured me on the boat and brought me back to the Palatial Room, were you certain I'd survive? That you'd found a loophole?"

"I'm not sure what's driving Savus, but he is defying the will of the Old Gods. I will not let anyone kill you."

I loosed the breath I'd been holding. I wanted to ask if he was protecting me because of the will of the Old Gods or because he actually liked me, but I reminded myself that it didn't really matter. As long as he was helping to keep me alive, I didn't need to know his motives.

I frowned at him. "You really had to leave it to the last moment to let me know you weren't going to cut off my head? You could have explained that a bit better on the way up the stairs."

He didn't respond, lapsing back into his characteristic silence. I swirled the wine in my glass, glaring at him. "Oh, you've lost your voice again. It's a wonderful way of avoiding things."

"I suppose I could always avoid things with constant chatter, like you do."

I glared at him, overcome by a desire to rile him up.

I kicked off my shoes and let the T-shirt ride up as I put my feet on the chair. I felt his gaze sliding up my legs, drinking me in until he reached my face. I licked my lips, and his eyes caught the movement. "Didn't Savus say you were supposed to punish me? Whip me, I think?"

Shadows billowed around him, and his body became eerily still. Ruadan, of course, said nothing, but his entire body tensed.

"No?" I went on. "Maybe a light spanking until I learn my lesson?"

I was teasing him, but I could also feel my chest flushing at the mental image.

His violet eyes darkened, and I smiled at the sight. Then, he lunged forward, planting his hands on the chair, one on either side of my hips. I leaned back, looking up at him as his magic washed over me. He wasn't touching me, but he was still boxing me in, in total control. His mouth hovered just inches from mine, his body practically vibrating with tension. His eyes were completely black as his demonic side took control. My knees slid open just a little, lips parting as heat swooped through my belly, and my pulse raced.

Then, he rose with a growl. He prowled away, with his hands clenched into fists.

"What happened to your human?" he asked, with his back to me. His voice had an edge to it. "She escaped from her room."

My good mood dampened as soon as I thought of Ciara. I could only hope she'd found a good place to hide out, and that maybe she could scrape together some food. "I guess her guard wasn't very good." *And that's all the information you're getting.*

I loosed a long breath, my pulse slowing again. "Ruadan. There's something I have to tell you. The gwyllion said something right before I killed her. She said Baleros was coming for me. That he wanted to make me his again. That's the second person now who said this. First the assassin, then the gwyllion. Plus, there were the sweets. I'm certain he's alive."

Ruadan's shadows seeped into the air around him like blood spilling into a field. "I believe he's still alive, too."

My chest tightened. "So why can't we track him? You hunted me down in a forest just by using my dreams. Why can't you track Baleros in the same way?"

"I've never been able to track him, to feel his dreams, or get into his mind. I've consulted with a fae elder, and I think I know what's happened."

"What?"

"We both saw his body ignite after I killed him. I think he may have sold his soul to the fire goddess."

"Emerazel?" I shook my head. "What would that mean?"

"The fire goddess is the ancient enemy of the god of night. That would explain why he's immune to my powers. It also would mean that he can't be killed. If he dies, the fire goddess revives him."

My jaw tightened, steeling my resolve. "There's a way to kill everyone. *Everyone.* And we will find a way to kill Baleros."

"We will. But first things first. You have another trial coming up. It's the final trial before a knight is chosen from the novices. And we both know what happens if you fail."

I knocked back the rest of my wine. I was getting a nice buzz going. "Right. What do I have to do?"

"What do you know about angels?"

I schooled my features to calm and poured myself another glass of wine. Talk about dredging up nightmares from the past. "The angels aren't on Earth anymore. So we don't need to worry about them. After the apocalypse, all the angels were exiled to the heavens. Driven off the earth forever. Everyone knows the story."

"Not exactly. Some of them have returned, and two of

the horsemen of the apocalypse never left. After we kill Baleros, they're next on my list. They're a scourge upon this earth."

I stared at him, my unease growing. "What's the harm in a few angels on Earth? They're hardly wreaking destruction these days."

A chill rippled through the room, and candles flickered in their sconces. The ice in the air had my teeth chattering.

"It doesn't matter what they're doing *these days.*" His deep, velvety voice had an edge of steel to it. "They're unnatural. They're responsible for everything that happened during the apocalypse. Millions of unnecessary deaths just to appease their egos. Men, women, children slaughtered across the globe. The angels—and worse, the horsemen—are the face of pure evil. They are death itself, and they must answer for their crimes."

I gripped the wineglass, ready to snap it. "Fine. So what's the mission? Hunt some angels?"

"Yes. A few cohorts of angels have returned to Earth. They're trying to learn to live as humans, to blend in. As you know, angels believe that humans are beasts. The angels have come to Earth to consort with humans in their most primitive, bestial state."

"In their most bestial state? What does that mean, exactly?" I asked.

"The task requires that you figure that out."

"And why, exactly, are they trying to live like primitive humans?"

"We think they're spies, possibly planning another apocalyptic assault on Earth. Except this time, they're disguising themselves. They've hidden their wings. They look like humans. They're trying to learn to behave like humans. We have to ferret them out before we find ourselves facing another apocalypse."

"If they're disguised, then how do you suggest that I pick out the humans from the angels?" I asked.

Ruadan lifted his hand. Purple light flickered between his fingertips, illuminating the beautiful planes of his face. "You know what happens if an angel indulges in earthly pleasure."

"He turns into a demon." A smile curled my lips. "I get it. I hit them with lust magic. The angels turn into demons. I kill them. Does that pretty much summarize it?"

"It's as simple as that. And I know you can kill. The hard part will be controlling the magic."

"But I still don't get a lumen stone?"

"Not until you become a knight. For now, you're considered a flight risk."

"Fine. So how do I distill this magical power?"

Ruadan pulled one of his swords off the wall. "We're leaving the Institute for this one. I don't want Maddan to know what we're planning."

He sheathed his sword, then turned his back to me. His magic rippled over my skin, and I stared as a portal opened in the floor—whirling dark waters flickered like starlight.

He turned to face me, and he gestured to the portal.

I jumped in, and the icy water rushed over my skin. As I sank deeper, it occurred to me that I didn't even ask him where we were going. I'd just simply jumped. Was I actually starting to trust him?

Ruadan's body plunged into the portal next to me, and we continued to sink, until at last, thin rays of moonlight pierced the water's surface. As my lungs burned, I kicked my legs, hurtling up toward the surface, faster and faster.

Then, the lip of a fountain came into view. I grasped on and hoisted myself up, catching my breath. Above me, water spilled from the mouth of a stone woman, splashing over the dark cobblestones. The air smelled intoxicating, heavy with sandalwood and jasmine.

Ruadan was already climbing from the fountain, his dark clothing dripping onto the cobblestones. "Lilinor, the vampire realm. We're safe. My half-brother Caine rules here with the king."

Ruadan's black shirt clung to my body like a second skin as I pulled myself over the lip of the fountain. We were standing on a narrow lane, where moonflowers and gardenias climbed the walls of rickety timber-framed buildings.

My gaze roamed upward, all the way to a crooked Gothic castle that loomed over the city. Amber lights burned in its narrow windows.

"Are we going up to that castle?" I asked.

Ruadan's damp, pale hair hung over his shoulders. "We don't need to go that far. We're going to practice in my friend's garden. It's nearby."

He began walking over the cobbles, and I followed behind him. We were heading for a grand house—it looked like a gabled Tudor mansion, with crisscrossing wood over white walls.

As we stood before the wooden door, Ruadan lifted the silver knocker, shaped like a hand. He knocked three times.

The clacking of footfalls penetrated the door. Then, it swung open. A buxom woman stood in the doorway, her dark hair piled high on her head. She wore a long lace gown. "Well if it isn't my favorite fae prince!"

CHAPTER 21

I blinked at him. "Prince?" Prince of what?

"Get the hells inside," she said. Her accent was American—Southern, in fact. "I need to hang a damn towel over that fountain so you don't trail all that water inside next time. Ruining my good hardwood floors with all that portal water."

She opened the door wide into a hall of dark wood, with an enormous stone fireplace burning bright.

Ruadan gave a slight bow. "We were hoping to use—"

"Shhhhh." The woman lifted a finger to her lips. "Where are your manners? From a royal family like you are, and you don't even know how to introduce a woman. No wonder you can't find yourself a damn wife." She turned her sharp, dark eyes to me. "I don't suppose you're his lover. Our grand fae prince here never has a lady friend."

"No, ma'am," I said. I had no idea where the *ma'am* came from. It just came out.

She stuck her finger in Ruadan's chest. "You're such a gods-damn fool, a man looking like you, warm-blooded man like you, can't find yourself a damn lady friend. Brooding all over the place, vowing silence, scaring everyone away with all your damn shadows. Making the lights flicker out when you walk into a room. No sensible lady is gonna want to go on a date with you if you keep making lights flicker out. They'll be tripping all over the place, running into walls, burning their pancakes. Can't see a damn thing when you're around with your moods."

Ruadan opened his mouth again to speak, but she silenced him with another jab to his chest.

"Making the air all cold with your tempers. At least you're not doing that stupid vow of silence anymore. Good. You know what won't help you kill people? Being silent. Gets you nowhere. Doesn't help you get a lady friend either."

Her sharp eyes turned to me, and she looked me up and down, letting out a low whistle. Then, to my horror, she stepped closer and poked at one of my breasts. "Good solid girl like this, good ample bosoms that a man could lay his head on at night, and she's not your lover. Gods-damned fool. Grown man like you, making lights flicker off. Six hundred years, still not remarried. Damn shame."

At last, her tirade seemed to have died out, and Ruadan gestured to me. "Elise, this is—"

She raised her hands. "Now I know you were married before, but that was a long damn time ago. Time to move on."

I stared at Ruadan. Well, I was certainly learning more about him now than I had in weeks of living with him. A prince, previously married.

And most shocking of all—he *actually* had friends.

Still, this last bit about his former wife seemed to have irked him, and a coolness fell over the room—an actual chill that raised goosebumps on my skin.

"Quit making my living room cold," shouted Elise. "What's the matter with you? Fool. That's what happens when you spend too much time celibate. Lose your temper over every damn thing, drive up everyone's heating bill with the cold air from your magic. No one wants to pay for that. No wonder you're still single."

Ruadan's body had stiffened, and he looked as if he were trying to restrain himself. Then, in a voice that was a little too smooth to be calm, he said, "This is my novice, Arianna, from London's Institute of the Shadow Fae. Arianna, this is Elise. She likes to go by Grandmother Elise. She's an old and dear friend."

"Grandmother?" I asked. "You don't...you don't look old enough to be a grandmother."

"I am two hundred seventy-eight years old. I have sired six generations of offspring." She beamed, apparently pleased with the introduction. When she smiled, her fangs glinted in the candlelight.

Ruadan narrowed his eyes at her windows. "You need to get light-blocking curtains on these windows, Elise. I've told you that before. You know what will happen if the sun rises and you've fallen asleep in the living room."

"Two hundred seventy-eight years old, and do you know how many times I've fallen asleep in the living room? Not once. Not once," she repeated.

"I'm coming back with curtains," he said, his voice a sharp command. "And I'm putting them up. Do not question me on this, Elise."

She rolled her eyes. "The prince makes an official decree. But you'd better not come in here with cheap curtains. Silk or nothing. Now what are y'all doing here? You need something to drink? I've got strawberry daiquiris, heavy on the rum."

"Yes." I smiled.

"No," Ruadan cut in. "But thank you. We're just hoping to borrow your orchard for some practice."

"You want to practice some of that Shadow Fae magic?"

She turned and began walking through the hall, heading for an oak door at the back.

We followed her.

"Now what kind of magic are you going to be practicing, just so I know?" she asked. "You're not going to be blowing up my apple trees, are you? I take very good care of my apple trees."

"No, Grandma Elise. Just lust magic." He said this like it was no big deal. In the same tone that one might discuss having a ham sandwich for lunch. *Oh, you know, just going out into your garden to magically channel sexual arousal all over your plants. Nothing awkward.*

She whirled, arching an eyebrow at Ruadan. "Grown man like you with lust magic. No wife. It's a gods-damned waste is what it is. You know all that pent-up sexual energy is no good for you. Human men blow themselves up over a thing like that. It's not natural. Gets your insides all clogged up and angry. Vow of celibacy. Making you all crazy, making the rooms go cold." She jabbed him in the shoulder. "People need to get themselves some hibbly jibbly."

She yanked the door open, glaring intensely at both of us with this hibbly jibbly directive.

When we stepped outside, the night wind whispered over my wet skin, making me shiver. I breathed in the powerful scent of apples. The air here felt moist and heavy.

Grandma Elise closed the door behind us.

We moved deeper into the garden—if it could even be called a garden. It was more a large, walled orchard. A stone bench sat in the center of it all, engraved with vines.

"You never told me you were a prince." I folded my arms. "Prince of what, exactly?"

His violet eyes pierced the darkness. After a long moment, he finally answered, "Emain."

I breathed in deeply. "So it is real. The place I dream about. The place in the library book."

"It's real." The intoxicating breeze of Lilinor lifted strands of his blond hair. Apart from that, he'd gone completely still, shadows thickening around him. "It's where the Shadow Fae High Council resides. It's where Baleros trained me, and where Grand Master Savus once lived."

I sucked in a sharp breath. I'd never known a bloody thing about Baleros's past. Of course I hadn't. *Knowledge is power.* "Emain? That's where Baleros is from? *That's* where he mentored you?"

"A legion of Shadow Fae protects Emain. It's part of our mission to keep the land secret, to convince everyone it's a myth. The realm is home to precious metals that demons would love to exploit. The Shadow Fae of Emain are some of the fiercest assassins in the world, and our training is harsher than most. In our youth, we scale mountains and swim across oceans—all for the purpose of training to protect the realm. We sacrifice to the Old Gods, but our mission is also to assassinate enemies of Emain. We kill demon and fae invaders and those we believe are planning attacks on the city."

I moved closer to him, desperate to learn more. The night air rushed over me. I kicked off my shoes, and the grass felt soft under my feet.

But I wasn't relaxing. I was hunting for information on Baleros, and I was going after this knowledge like a foxhound scenting blood. "How did Baleros end up in London? Why did he leave Emain?"

"You're not going to let me get away with silence, are you?"

"You bet your life I won't." My fingers tightened into fists. I needed to know the truth about all of this.

"Baleros was my mentor in Emain hundreds of years ago, when I was young. He left Emain three centuries ago. He joined the London Institute, but he chafed against the authority of Grand Master Savus. Baleros fled the Institute in the 1800s, and he began trafficking stolen magical items. After the apocalypse, it wasn't enough for him. Fifteen years ago, he returned to Emain and tried to seize control of the realm. To become king. He slaughtered Queen Macha. Shot her through with iron arrows, burnt her body until nothing was recognizable except her crown." Shadows darkened his eyes, and the temperature around us cooled until my breath frosted in front of my face.

I'd moved closer to Ruadan, and his face had taken on a haunted quality. My chest ached for him, and I had the strongest urge to wrap my arms around him. "Queen Macha —your mother?"

"Yes. I was the one who found her in her room. But when Baleros realized none of the warriors supported his coup, he fled Emain. I vowed silence until I achieved his death. I joined the London Institute. Baleros was top of my kill list. But I could never track him, and now, I know why. The goddess of flames protects him. The ancient enemy of my grandfather."

I sucked in a deep breath. "And while you were hunting Baleros, he was keeping me below ground as a slave, less than a mile away from the Institute." I swallowed hard. "What was your mother like, before she died?"

"Strong. A warrior. She was small, but powerful. She rode a horse faster than anyone in the kingdom. She spoke sixteen languages and swore like a gutter tramp." He frowned. "No offense."

"I actually didn't take offense until you said 'no offense.' Anyway, your mum sounds brilliant." I hugged myself, chilly in my damp dress. "Why are you telling me about Emain if it's such a deep secret?"

"Because I know you'll keep it."

"I will." The idea that he trusted me sparked a bit of warmth inside. I fought the urge to ask him about his wife. Curiosity burned in me, but I'd seen how he reacted to Grandma Elise, driving up her heating bill with his coldness.

CHAPTER 22

"You will become a knight," Ruadan said. "The Old Gods desire it. You will live. And you will help me find Baleros. But first, you have to pass tomorrow's trial. You'll need to identify the angels and kill each one of them." He held out his palm, and a silver ring gleamed in his hand. It glowed faintly with violet light. "I've imbued this with my magic. You'll need to learn to channel it."

I picked up the ring from his palm and slid it onto my finger. As I did, a jolt of heat raced through my blood. I became acutely aware of Ruadan's T-shirt clinging to my body, my breasts peaking in the cold breeze. My mind flashed with a vivid memory of my dream about Ruadan. I wanted him to lose control of himself, to pin me up against a tree. Already, the blood was rushing out of my head and making it hard for me to think.

"You need to control it." His magic licked at my skin, stroking up the back of my spine like a silky fingertip, an invisible caress. "Not the other way around."

My pulse raced, my breathing quickening. "I'm perfectly

in control." I stared at my fingertips, which now flickered with violet light. Without realizing what I was doing, I reached for Ruadan's sodden shirt. I pulled him close, and he stared down at me. He felt *warm.* I slid my hand up his powerful torso.

"Control it." His voice was a blade wrapped in silk, and it only made me want to touch him more.

I rested my head against his muscled chest, looking up at his perfect face. My fingers slid inside the hem of his shirt, over his muscled abs, and I heard him gasp, his muscles tensing. His skin was soft, with pure steel underneath. I ran my hand higher up his chest, feeling his muscles. He leaned down, his breath warming the shell of my ear. He wasn't pushing me away.

Fifteen years he'd been with London's Institute. Fifteen years since he'd had sex. He must be desperate for it.

When I closed my eyes, the scent of apples grew stronger. A vision rose in my mind of an orchard on a rocky slope—Emain. Someone had decorated the tree branches with candles that flickered in the darkness like stars, and a distant drum beat through my blood. I stalked through the trees, hunting...

Ruadan pulled my hand off his body, his grip like iron on my fingers.

I gritted my teeth, trying to gain control of myself. "What the hells was that vision?"

"What vision?" he asked.

"It was Emain, with candles in the trees, and a drumbeat."

A silence stretched out between us. "I think you saw one of my memories. It must be carried by the magic I gave you."

"You were hunting something."

"A woman. It was a fertility festival."

I shook my head, willing my body to cool down. "Right. You know most people just get drunk and watch TV, but I do like the candles and drums. I take it the Emain Shadow Fae were not celibate?"

"Fortunately, no."

It took me a moment to realize that I'd grabbed onto his shirt again and pulled him close, arching my neck to look up at him. Gods, I wanted to be there in Emain for that festival, to be hunted by Ruadan, pulled down in the dewy grass. I wanted Ruadan's powerful hands to rip my clothes off while I writhed beneath him…

Through our damp clothes, his body warmed mine. I clenched my fists, still clutching his shirt, and I looked up into his eyes. He gripped my waist once more, and his heated gaze burned right into me. I felt an overwhelming urge to pull my wet T-shirt up higher. Darkness slid through his eyes as my arousal started to affect him, too. Even if he was supposed to be celibate, the incubus in him was responding.

When the chilly wind hit my thighs, raising goosebumps, I realized that I actually *had* inched the shirt up to my waist.

Now, I was desperate to kiss him, to feel his tongue sliding against mine. My pulse raced.

I wanted to get down on the damp ground with him, and…

Focus, Arianna.

I expected him to be annoyed, because so far, I was completely failing to effectively channel the magic. But I *had to* prove to him that I could do this. His faith in me was not misplaced.

I willed my heartbeat to slow, still staring into his eyes. And as I gazed up at him, I saw something new there. Something almost possessive. Or was it protective?

"How, exactly, do I control it?" I asked.

"It's the magic of life," he said, his voice an erotic rumble through my belly. "And the opposite of life—"

With an iron will, I forced myself to take a step back from him. "Death. You want me to think about death?"

"Fill yourself with darkness. It will help you control the power as it dampens the lust magic."

A dark smile curled my lips. "Oh, believe me. Death is something that comes naturally to me."

While the lust magic continued to heat up my body, I closed my eyes, summoning my worst memories of destruction: fae blood staining the soil, bodies lying at my feet in the arena. Vacant eyes. Hearts ripped, still beating, from bodies. Like ink spilling through water, the darkness pushed out some of the lust magic from my core, moving it to my extremities.

"There," said Ruadan, his voice wrapping around me like velvet. He traced his fingertip from my shoulder, down my arm, and tingles raced in its wake. "I can see it moving through your body, the way it should."

I took a deep breath, in control once more, and I stepped away to look at my hand. Violet magic throbbed at my fingertips.

"Good."

The approval in his eyes made me smile—at least for a moment, until I mentally excoriated myself for caring so much what he thought. I shouldn't want his approval as much as I did.

"Of course it's good." I stood tall. "The Amazon Terror is nothing less than amazing."

"That's a ridiculous name."

"Okay, *Wraith.*"

"You'll notice I do not refer to myself in the third person. In any case, now you'll need to learn to hurl the magic at a target."

"Right."

"I'm going to move through the trees. Try to hit me with it."

"Won't you be overcome by an overwhelming desire for hibbly jibbly?"

He shook his head. "No. The magic comes from me. I'll be fine."

With a hissing sound, he disappeared, leaving only a whorl of shadows behind.

I tracked his movements through the trees, and he slowed to a normal walking pace. I looked down at the pulsing violet magic at the tips of my fingers, and I flung back my arm to try to hurl it at him. Except, on the back stroke, the magic flew off my fingertips. I watched as it soared through a glass window into Grandma Elise's house.

I sucked in a deep breath. Looked like she might be in for an interesting evening.

Once that burst of magic had left my body, the lust magic began surging again, heating my skin. Even from across the orchard, I could feel Ruadan's unmistakable masculine allure. I closed my eyes as I walked barefoot through the dewy grasses, breathing in the sensual scents of the orchard. The night air felt heavy, and the wet T-shirt slid against my bare legs. My breasts, too, seemed fuller in the shirt. If I took off all my clothes, could I tempt him to hunt me?

My gaze slid over every inch of Ruadan, the moonlight washing over his muscled body, his powerful arms. I could imagine the feel of his mouth on my throat, my bare legs wrapped around his waist. Molten heat surged, and my hardened nipples chafed against the wet shirt.

The rush of cold air over my bare thighs told me that once again I'd started hiking up my T-shirt. *Death. Blood, broken bodies, rotting flesh, vacant eyes.*

Darkness spooled out through my limbs, chasing away

the sensual magic until it pulsed from my fingertips once again.

I lifted my hand, taking care to throw the magic faster this time. It hit Ruadan in the chest, his back arched, and a smile curled his lips. Then, magic surged through my blood once more, and erotic heat stroked over my skin, pooling between my legs.

I closed my eyes, letting my body fill with the dizzying weightlessness of death, until the darkness pushed the violet magic out to my extremities again.

"This time," said Ruadan, "when you throw it, try to toss it into the air and disperse it over the orchard."

"How do I do that?" I asked.

"It's all in the throw. Splay your fingers. Just practice."

I hurled the magic into the air, my body rocked by each burst. It took me four or five tries until I could flick my fingers in just the right way that the magic spread out, raining down over the orchard.

Ruadan prowled closer to me. When he was only a few feet away, I threw more violet magic at him. His back arched as it hit him. All at once, the magic recharged in my body, and heat arced through my core until I could think of nothing but how my naked body would feel sliding against his.

I grabbed him by the shirt, then pushed him down to the stone bench. Without entirely realizing what I was doing, I straddled him, my shirt riding up, exposing my panties. His fingers clamped around my waist, hungry and possessive. I leaned in to kiss him, my tongue licking his. My hips rocked against him.

The kiss deepened, and my breasts brushed against his chest. His fingers slid up my wet thighs, higher and higher, until he was gripping my bum. When I pulled away to look into his eyes, they'd turned completely black with the unrestrained lust of an incubus. His magic slid over my skin, stroking me all over.

He shoved his hand into my hair, and he pulled my head back, exposing my neck. His kiss seared my throat, and my back arched further. With his tight grip on my hair and my waist, he was in complete control of me now, and my body was on fire. My thighs clenched around him.

But something he'd said rang in the hollows of my mind. *Angels were never supposed to be on this earth…they are the face of true evil, and they must answer for their crimes. A scourge…*

My blood turned to ice, and I pulled away from him, jumping to my feet. I smoothed down my damp T-shirt, taking a long, slow breath. I forced my pulse to slow. "Let's not do that again." My voice sounded sharper than I wanted it to.

For just a moment, I thought I saw a flash of vulnerability in his eyes, and I felt the impact of it like a pang in my chest. Then, his gaze shuttered.

Now that'd I'd stood up, I was freezing.

"You're right," he said. "Of course. And it seems like you've mastered the skill we came here to practice." He rose, and his eyes faded from deep, animalistic black to their usual cold violet. He wasn't looking at me anymore. "Tomorrow, when the trial begins, you will need to hunt down the enclave of angels. Use the lust magic." Already, he was moving for the house, eyes straight ahead. He did not want to look at me at all. "You'll see the angels begin to transform before your very eyes. Then, you just need to slaughter them."

"I take it you don't think I need any extra lessons in slaughtering demons."

"I have no concerns about your ability to kill. Just make sure you get there before Maddan does. Don't leave anyone for him to slaughter. If you succeed in this trial, Grand

Master Savus will have to accept that the Old Gods have chosen you. It will be over for Maddan, or Savus will lose his crown for good."

He pulled open the door to Grandmother Elise's house.

She stood in the center of the room in a cream bathrobe, her cheeks flushed. She took a sip of a pink cocktail, her cleavage on full display. She *really* didn't look like a grandmother.

She crossed to Ruadan, swishing her hips. "Big strong man like you, going to waste." She gripped him by the belt of his pants and pulled him closer. Her drink sloshed as he slammed into her. "I'll tell you what, Prince of Misery, I will ride you hard until I put a smile on that face." She nodded at me. "Your friend can come too. I'm not greedy. I will share."

He disengaged her hand from his trousers. "Thank you for your orchard, Grandmother Elise. I'll visit again soon to fix your curtains."

Ruadan ushered me toward the door with his hand on the small of my back, quickening his pace.

"I want more than just curtains when you get back here. Gods-damned waste," she muttered as we left.

CHAPTER 23

Maddan and I stood before the Institute's gates, and our mentors flanked us. At least His Royal Twattiness had the good sense to leave the crown behind. I wore a black dress and boots—the dress short enough that I could easily run.

For our angel-hunting mission, I wore a sword slung over my back—my favorite weapon. Ruadan's ring sat tucked in my pocket, and I was ready to slip it on when I found the angels. I was keeping it hidden for now. No need to let Maddan know what I had planned.

This time, we had to hunt down our targets on our own. All I knew was that the angels were trying to live like primitive humans to learn about human culture, and that they wanted to infiltrate our world again— covertly. But it wasn't much to go on. They could be hiding, disguised as humans, anywhere in London. I had no idea what to make of the whole "primitive" idea.

I glanced at Maddan again, and the violet lumen stone glowing around his neck. He'd be able to leap all over the city with that thing. Unfortunately, I was stuck moving around in much more mundane ways: walking or crammed between drunk, sweaty men on the Tube.

As I turned it over in my mind, mist roiled over the ground, bubbling like a cauldron brew. Footfalls echoed off the stone, and Grand Master Savus shifted out of the shadows and into the moonlight. His silver crown gleamed on his head—now slightly restored. Apparently, his failure to execute me had him back in the Old Gods' favor.

"Tonight," he began, "You must act like real trackers, the way the Shadow Fae must track in real life. Somewhere, in the great city of London, the angels have made it their mission to learn the primitive ways of the human species. These angelic spies seek to live like primal human beasts, connecting themselves to the earth. They want to study the wild impulses of the human race."

I frowned, fairly certain they'd arrived several thousand years too late for that sort of caveman thing. Then again, if the Millwall football team lost, they might be in luck.

"We're not telling you the targets' location." Grand Master Savus's silver hair flitted in the breeze. "Your task is simple. Find the angels, and kill them." Then, Savus glared at me, his silver eyes glinting. "I will be watching your every move through my scrying mirror. Ruadan will follow you to make sure you don't attempt an escape. I'm sure you understand by now that you cannot escape him."

Nope. He finds me through my sex dreams.

The gate groaned open to a stony esplanade before the Institute. In a blur of dark shadows, Maddan was off, the wind whooshing past me as he dashed away. I had to hope that he had no idea what the hells he was doing.

Now, how to find the angels? I closed my eyes, letting my mind go blank for a moment.

Mentally, I reviewed what Savus had said. *Primitive. Primal. Beasts. Wild. Connected to the earth.*

As I rolled the words over and over, a seed of an idea took root in my mind, until I knew *exactly* where to start.

* * *

IN THE MILDEWED hall of my old squat, I knocked on Uncle Darrell's door. A shuffling noise sounded on the other side, and then the door creaked open.

As soon as I saw his face, I knew I'd made the right decision. He stood before me wearing a bicycle helmet with stag's horns duct-taped to either side. In addition to the antlers, he wore a wool poncho with no trousers, and about forty-seven crystal necklaces.

He beamed. "Arianna! What happened to you? Did you hear all the rumors that the spell-slayers got you? I told people, I said no—" His gaze darted to Ruadan, who stood behind me, and he fell silent.

Then, he dropped to his knees. "Oh ancient one! Oh masterful fae! Being of eternal light!"

"Darkness, really," I corrected him. "Never mind. Darrell, please stand up. We need your help."

As he rose, the tips of his antlers knocked into the top of the doorframe, and he winced, straightening them. "Took a lot of time to put this together," he muttered.

It smelled *heavily* of spliffs inside.

He brushed off his hands on his poncho. "What can I help you with, then?"

"I'm looking for a…some kind of primal, primitive event. I don't know what you'd call it. People acting like beasts? Connecting to the earth?"

"The midsummer festival. Yeah, I'm on my way now, actually. Men only to start, but we could use a real fae, like your friend here. You'll really connect to the earth; do you know what I mean?" His lip curled in a "hurts so good" face.

"Feel Mother Nature's glorious embrace like a…" He grunted and made a cupping motion with his hands, and I tried not to imagine what the gesture was supposed to represent. "Do you know what I mean?"

Ruadan just stood there, his arms folded, darkening the hallway with his magic. The air misted in front of my face, and I thought of Grandma Elise complaining about her heating bill.

I scratched my cheek. "Yeah he's not into that so much. I think he'll be hanging back, actually. You said it was men only?"

He scrunched up his face. "It's sort of a man thing, you know? Recharging our testosterone from the earth's roots. Really reconnect to our balls." He raised his eyebrows at Ruadan, as if hoping for some sort of approval.

The lights in the hallway flickered on and off.

Darrell's antlers clacked against the doorframe. "So anyway, the idea is that the primal drumbeats will attract females, who will mate with us like beasts."

I nodded. "Right. Seems reasonable. Maybe I could just… be in the vicinity for when that happens."

He nodded enthusiastically, antlers wobbling. "Yeah. I like it. We will celebrate like the ancient primordial power of the earth. We'll populate her flesh with our seed. Right." He clapped his hands together. "Let's take the District Line. It'll bring us right there."

WE RODE THE OLD, creaking Tube train across town. Ruadan sat at the far end of the car, cloaked in shadows, occasionally provoking screams from anyone who entered near him.

Uncle Darrell and I sat in the center of the car, and he pulled out his bongo drum to serenade me for the journey.

Get me in the mood. I closed my eyes, trying to mentally summon a happier place, which—given the grim circumstances—included the Palatial Room.

As he drummed on the bongos, singing along, one of his helmet antlers caught on a silver pole. "Fucking hell. The way they make these bloody trains. Honestly." He shook his head at me, as if I were about to commiserate with him about the lack of consideration for helmet-antlers in the Tube's design.

At last, the train pulled up to Richmond Park station, the brakes screeching as it ground to a halt. Darrell snatched up his drum, with one hand on his helmet. The doors slid open, and Uncle Darrell carefully ducked to avoid catching his antlers on the ceiling on the way out. Ruadan slipped out another door, keeping his distance from us. I wasn't sure if that was mentor protocol, or just the sheer embarrassment of walking around in public with Uncle Darrell.

Darrell reached into his bag and pulled out a bottle. He unscrewed the top, then handed it to me. "Try it."

I took a sip, then immediately spit the rancid liquid onto the pavement. "Fucking hells. What is that?"

"Fermented goat milk. I make it myself."

I gagged, not entirely sure he even knew what "fermented" meant.

Through an open gate, we crossed into a dark, grassy park. I glanced behind me, catching a glimpse of Ruadan's bright violet eyes. He was still hanging back—just watching. Making sure I didn't escape.

"I'm afraid this is where I've got to leave you," said Darrell. "The men are gathering. Can you hear the drums? Can you feel the beat of primal life in your blood? We'll mate soon."

"So should just I wait a bit then?"

He shrugged. "Yeah, just give it a few minutes. Let the drums lure you."

One of his antlers started to sag, and he held it up with his hand as he turned and walked off in the darkness.

I closed my eyes, tuning into the distant sound of the drums. After giving him a few moments, I began following Darrell at a distance, while scanning the park for signs of Maddan. I sniffed the air. I couldn't smell the prince, but I smelled something new—the scent of iron. The metal of the angels.

I slid the silver ring onto my finger, and my back arched at the rush of magic through my body.

Time to watch some angels fall from grace.

CHAPTER 24

I walked barefoot over forest soil on my way through Richmond Park. Moonlight beamed over tall grasses. A distant drumbeat boomed in my gut, stirring my blood—but not for lust, as Darrell had hoped. No, I was in a fighting mood.

The drumbeat grew louder as I approached a clearing. Someone had tied ribbons from the trees surrounding the glade. Through the trunks, I caught a glimpse of a bonfire. I'd come to the right place.

I glanced down at the violet magic twisting between my fingertips.

Sheltered behind an oak, I peered through the trees into the clearing. There, men dressed in loincloths danced around the fire, Uncle Darrell among them. He wore bells on his ankles and wrists.

As I stared at them, footfalls crunched behind me. I whirled, shoving my glowing hand into my pocket. There, standing behind me, I found a man. His potbelly hung over his loincloth, and he'd painted his face with blue streaks.

Moonlight shone on his bald scalp. By his smell, he was definitely human.

He pushed his spectacles up on his nose. "Oh, hello there. The, uh, the shaman said the drumbeat might attract mates. Primal thing, innit. Are you here to mate?"

"No, I'm not here to mate," I said quietly. There was no way in hells I wanted to hit this guy with lust magic. This conversation had started off bad enough as it was.

"You are, actually." He leaned against the tree.

"Don't tell me what I think, fuckwit." My voice came out louder and angrier than I'd aimed for.

He held up his hands. "Sorry. I was told that what women really want is to be controlled and protected by an alpha. We went stag hunting tonight to connect to our primitive selves."

I brushed my fingertips over the strap on my chest, tempted to use my sword on him. This man was wasting my time.

"It's in the hormones," he went on. "Females like a man who can provide. I read a book about it. Men are supposed to plant their seed in a harem of younger females. It's biology, innit." He cleared his throat. "Unfortunately, turns out, a stag is very hard to shoot with a bow and arrow, so I can't say we caught one. Derek caught an arrow in the leg, and Kevin injured himself with the bowstring. Someone brought a goat, but it ran away before we could shoot it. The bloody thing ate our cheesy biscuits, too, and I'd really been looking forward to them."

I was still mentally ticking over the moral issues with just cutting off his head.

"Anyway, how do we proceed?" he went on. "I'm not entirely comfortable with human mating rituals. Should I buy you a sausage or another type of food item? A box of cereal? I could get you a kebab or something and then we could have some sex while I try to bite your neck from behind, like a lion?" He made his hands into claws.

I blinked. "You're not…human?" I could have sworn he was. He smelled human, and he seemed too feeble to be anything else.

A loud chortle. "Oh, I am! Of course. I just seriously don't know how normal human mating rituals work. I was told something about providing food and biting, to assert dominance."

I glanced back at the shamans. Uncle Darrell was gripping the stag's antlers on his head. "None of these people know how normal humans behave. You're learning from the wrong people." Which would make it all the more difficult to pick out the angels among them, unless I just rained the magic down on top of them.

Another human man lumbered behind him. This one had strapped cardboard to his arms, and he'd glued the cardboard with orange and yellow feathers. He wore a bird mask pushed up on his head, and he gnawed on a chicken wing. "Oh, heya, Martin. Did you lure a female for mating?'

Martin scratched his nose. "Yeah, I'm not sure she's going for it. I'm not really sure what's going wrong."

"Did you tell her about the lion-biting?" His friend frowned, perplexed. "And the kebab?"

Martin blinked. "I did, Gareth, yeah."

"I'm not going for it," I confirmed.

The bird man spread out his wings. "I'm actually a gladiator myself."

There was no way in hells this man was a gladiator. He'd die within seconds.

"In World of Warcraft," he added. "How'd you like to mate with a phoenix? Spiritually connect to the beginning and the end of the universe?"

I shook my head. "Birds don't have penises, so…"

His face fell. "They don't?"

"Only ducks, but..." I let the sentence trail off. I'd wasted enough time with these two. "You know what? Never mind. Also, sorry about this."

"About what?" asked Martin.

Rapid-fire, I slammed my fist twice into the side of Martin's head, knocking him unconscious. Bird-man started to emit a little yelp, but I pivoted, bashing his skull with my left hand.

The two human men fell to the ground, their chests still moving. Good enough.

I turned back to the clearing. With the ring on my finger, I summoned the lust magic until it crackled at my fingertips, pulsing with violet. I hurled it into the air, flicking my fingers at the end of the throw. The violet magic dispersed, spreading out over the festival. Pure lust rained down on the men. Within moments, they were groaning, rubbing their chests. Uncle Darrell got down on the ground to defile the soil once again. Overhead, ravens circled us, wildly cawing.

Hiding behind the oak, I pulled my sword from its sheath, staring as some of the men began to transform. Dark, leathery wings sprouted from their backs. Their skin scaled over, reds and greens glistening in the moonlight. Claws and talons sprouted from their hands. Lightning cracked the sky, a flash of white light illuminating horns.

The breath left my lungs. I'd heard of angels falling, but I'd never seen it before. My lip curled. It was repulsive.

The Institute had been exactly right. Angels *were* trying to infiltrate the human race once again, an insidious attempt to start another apocalypse. I hadn't thought angels were much of a threat these days, but apparently they were. We had to let these celestial beings know that if they tried coming to Earth, they would all die like mortals.

Lightning speared the sky again, thunder rumbling. I

scanned the crowd, counting the demons among them. Eight in total.

What I hadn't expected was for the demons to immediately turn on the humans, hungry for flesh. Their teeth and claws sunk into the humans' skin. Inwardly, I cursed Ruadan. Maybe this hadn't been the best plan. The pleasurable groans had turned to terrified screams.

In any case, I was about to dispatch all the fallen angels. And Maddan hadn't even arrived yet. Things were looking up for the Amazon Terror.

With my sword drawn, I rushed into the clearing.

As I did, a demon with iridescent skin and shimmering wings spotted me. He raced for me, dark magic spilling from his body, snarling as he ran.

I swung my sword in a controlled arc and struck it through his neck.

The scent of demon blood drew the others closer. Seven demons surrounded me, but at least they'd stopped ripping into the humans.

I sliced my blade through the air, pivoting rapidly to keep them at bay.

The human men were running away from the scene, shrieking. I caught a glimpse of Uncle Darrell pulling up his trousers as he tried to flee.

A demon clawed at me from behind, slashing into the flesh of my back. I whirled, bringing down my sword hard into his shoulder. I nearly cleaved his torso, but I couldn't quite drive it in deep enough. The fucker was still standing. Another vicious slash at my back, and I whirled again, driving my sword through the demon's heart.

Pain splintered my upper body, but I tried to block it out, to focus on the fight. I'd been outnumbered before, but six on one wasn't ideal. At least they didn't have weapons beyond their own claws.

My own primal instincts began to take over, my blood sparking with adrenaline. They'd come to Earth to witness primitive beasts, and I could show them what they wanted to see.

I had to move quickly, whirling as they lunged for me. I fended them off with parries from my sword. When teeth sank into my neck from behind, I nearly dropped my weapon, and blood pounded in my skull. Losing my sword would be death. Luckily, I managed to keep a tight grip on it, and I slammed my elbow hard into the demon's ribs. Then I kicked the next demon who was lunging for me.

Battle fury raced through my blood, my heartbeat slamming against my ribs. Strength imbued my limbs, as memories of my gladiator days whispered through my blood. The warrior in me was coming out to play. I was no longer Arianna. I was the Amazon Terror, steel and teeth, fists and rage. I didn't feel pain or fear, only cold fury. The demons were after my blood, and I'd fend them off with the tip of my blade.

My senses had tuned into the demons' smallest movements—their labored breaths, their grunts, the shifting of their feet, their wings beating the air. As they clawed at me, I had a mental map of their positions.

I thrust my sword through another demon's chest. *Five to one.*

A clawed hand raked at my back, deeper this time. I whirled. My sword carved right through his neck, blood spurting. *Four to one.*

If these had been archangels, I would've been screwed. Luckily, they were regular old angels.

I was breathing faster now, my heart racing. The demons had started screeching, frantic with a lust for death. One of them grabbed me by the hair, pulling my head back. His teeth clamped into my collarbone, and pain splintered my neck. I brought my foot up hard into his groin, then swung for the demons again, my action more wild this time.

I tightened my grip on the sword, trying to summon the battle fury that would give me energy, and would block out the pain. As blood poured from my body, my attacks grew clumsier. Dizziness clouded my mind.

CHAPTER 25

My mouth had gone dry. Blood loss? Somewhere, in the back of my mind, I was wondering what Ruadan would do if it looked like I was about to die. Would he intervene?

Sharp talons seared my side, and I swung again, slicing my sword right into the demon's ribs. I drove it through to his heart.

Three to one.

I was floundering, badly injured. I needed a new tactic to finish this fight. A quick scan of the surroundings didn't highlight anything I could use against them. But maybe distraction alone would help.

Baleros's sixteenth law of power: Use the element of surprise.

I shifted my sword to my left hand, summoning the lust magic with my right. I flung the violet magic into the air, and it rained down on us. As it hit me, my skin heated, and my mind flashed with images of Ruadan.

Gods damn it. I'd distracted myself, too.

Still, it had worked, and the demons stopped trying to kill me. I tried not to look at the unfortunate demonic bulges they were sporting in their trousers, and I attempted to block out the memory of how Ruadan had looked without a shirt on.

Death. Think of death.

Darkness pooled in my body, racing through my limbs like an opiate, pushing the lust magic out to my extremities.

Three distracted demons left to go. With a sharpened focus, I cut my sword into the first one, hacking off his head.

Six down.

I whirled, stabbing another in the chest. I drove my blade through his heart. When the last one lunged for me, I ran my sword through his abdomen. He fell, and I drew out my blade. Thick, sticky blood coated the steel, dripping onto the earth.

Eight down. Euphoria bubbled in my chest. I was going to be knighted, at last. I'd finally be safe.

With my opponents all dead, I gripped my side. They'd torn some of my flesh to shreds, ripping through old scars to make new ones.

I speared the earth with the sword, then knelt down in front of it. A sacrifice for the Old Gods, who seemed to favor me.

"Old Gods," I mumbled, dizzy from the blood loss. "This is for you. A sacrifice and whatnot. You're welcome."

A strong hand helped me up. I rose, practically falling, into Ruadan's chest. He steadied me.

"You did well." His rich voice soothed me.

I closed my eyes, leaning against him. "I'd say so. They're all dead. None left for Maddan."

Ruadan's body tensed, and when I looked up at his face, my pulse started to race. I could feel his heartbeat quickening through his shirt. His eyes had darkened, and he stared across the park.

The air cooled. Ruadan pulled away from me, letting me

stand on my own. I gripped my side, where one of the demons had slashed into my flesh.

"What do you see?" I asked.

"Grand Master Savus is here, and he's not alone."

"To knight me, or what?"

"He should be knighting you. It was the final trial, and you clearly won. But the ceremony usually happens at the Institute."

Mist had grown thicker in the park, curling in steamy tendrils off the grass. Slowly, my eyes adjusted to the dark and the fog, and I shuddered at the sight of a small legion marching closer. Their silver armor shone in the moonlight, cowls pulled over their heads.

"Who are they?" I asked.

"That's the mist army." Ruadan stepped in front of me. The gesture would have annoyed me, except I was losing so much blood that I frankly needed the protection.

Savus stepped out from the mist, his silver hair tucked neatly beneath his crown—the metal now rotten and black. "Arrest her."

Ruadan's dark magic billowed from his body, tingeing the mist with darkness. The air around us grew so cold that the dew on the grass turned to crystallized frost. I hugged myself, shivering.

"Arrest her for what?" asked Ruadan. His deep voice held a threat of violence that slid right through my bones.

I gritted my teeth. Considering Grand Master Savus had brought an entire mist legion with him, we weren't going to fight our way out of this.

Savus's serene smile was like a single claw up my spine. And when I scanned the army behind him, my heart only beat faster. Fog pulsed around them, as if someone were blowing it through a bellows. Their eyes glowed with silver.

Savus tapped a leather-gloved hand against his silver

fingertips. "The excuses about the reaping dagger. The lust magic driving her mad. That's not what happened." He cut a sharp look to Ruadan. "And you know it. You lied for her, didn't you? I already had you flogged once for failing to kill her like I'd asked. I knew you favored the gutter fae. Now, I've learned you lied to me. Your mother would be so disappointed. A traitor to the Shadow Fae. All because a pretty demi-fae caught your eye."

My body felt weak, and I faltered. Savus had asked Ruadan to kill me? I supposed that was one way to get around angering the Old Gods. Have someone else do your dirty work for you. But Ruadan had refused. In fact, he'd taken a flogging for me, and he hadn't even told me. I guess that explained the deep scars I'd seen on the back of his arms.

But if Ruadan hadn't told Savus about Baleros, who had?

Ruadan's dark magic snaked through the air. "Baleros was threatening her friend, and Arianna was trying to protect her. Our role is to protect, isn't it? That's what she was doing."

To the right of the mist army, another man was moving. The fog curled around his body. Except, he wasn't part of the army. By his red hair and glittering crown, I recognized him as Maddan.

"You can't turn on her now." Ruadan's voice boomed through the fog. "The Old Gods have chosen her. She successfully completed the task. She identified and slaughtered all the angels. Angel blood coats her sword. Look at the state of your crown."

Maddan crossed to Ruadan, his face beet-red. "Lies!" he shrieked. He'd dipped his sword in blood at some point, and it dripped off his blade. "I won the task by default. The incubus was helping her. Anyone could see that he was helping her. He gave her his magic. This is not the work of the Old Gods. This is the work of Ruadan. I killed an angel on my own, without the benefit of his help."

"You didn't kill a single angel," I shouted. "You weren't even here."

He lifted his sword. "You left one of them alive. I finished him."

Grand Master Savus straightened. "Perhaps the Old Gods do favor the demi-fae. But she came from Baleros, and we cannot trust her. Clearly, she cannot be a Shadow Fae. The Shadow Fae must trust one another, and she is a spy. We will keep her in the Palatial Room until we decide a further course of action."

Ruadan's dark magic roiled around him like a storm, and the temperature plummeted. His pale hair whipped around his head. "Who told you about Baleros?" he asked, in a tone that turned my own blood to ice.

"Arrest her," Savus repeated.

At his order, a line of mist soldiers began marching for me. Injured, I was too weak to fight them. Ruadan had no chance of slaughtering them all. And yet, for some insane reason, he decided to try. As the soldiers closed in around us, he drew his blade, moving like a hurricane wind. He was a blur of shadows and speed, furiously carving into shadow soldiers. But it didn't seem as if a blade could hurt them. With each attack of his sword, the soldiers dissipated like smoke.

When a new line of mist soldiers raised their bows, arrows nocked, my mind started to go blank. That familiar darkness—the weightlessness of falling—spilled through my blood.

I held it back the best I could. If I unleashed my true self, everyone would die—Ruadan included.

The archers launched their arrows, all aimed at Ruadan.

He shadow-leapt, shifting position, but one of the arrows still slammed into his chest. He fell back to the earth.

My world tilted as I recognized the dark sheen of iron. An inch or two to the right, and it would have pierced his heart, killing him.

I stared at him, my own heart squeezing in my chest as the mist soldiers surrounded me. They gripped my arms, dragging me away from him. What would happen to him? He'd risen up against Savus—committed treason. Would they kill the prince of Emain?

Rough hands of mist pulled me down, smothering me, until my world went black.

CHAPTER 26

I woke to find myself back in the Palatial Room. This time, no one had thought to leave me with my bug-out bag. Rough stone bit into my back, and the stench nearly overpowered me. An irregular dripping noise echoed off the dungeon walls.

My wounds felt like they were ripping me apart. "I'm getting really irritated with this place," I muttered.

"Arianna?" Ruadan's voice wended through the dark, a velvety caress on my skin.

My chest unclenched at the sound of his voice. "Ruadan? Are you okay?"

"I've been better." His voice sounded strained.

"Did they get the iron out of your chest?"

"No. But it missed my heart."

I winced. The agony must be excruciating. In fact, it must be poisoning his blood even now.

"I don't suppose you can *Wraith* your way out of here," I said.

"Not with all the iron piercing me. I hardly have any magic left. How are your wounds?"

Someone had snuffed out all the candles, and I couldn't even see my injuries in the darkness. But oh gods, I could feel them. Pain lashed me from all sides. "I've been better," I said. "The last time I was in here, I dreamt of…" I didn't want to say the word *Emain* in case a guard was listening in. "I dreamt of apple orchards on a rocky slope. I'm not sure how I slept so well in here. I slept the entire time." Only now was I starting to put the pieces together. As a demigod of the night, Ruadan had sleep magic at his fingertips. "That was you, wasn't it?"

He didn't answer, but now I was certain that it had been him. A prince of Emain, who'd sent me calming dreams so I could rest in this horrible place. "They were nice dreams," I added.

"When I was a boy, before I joined the Shadow Fae, I spent all day in that orchard. My brothers and I played soldiers, hunting each other with wooden swords."

"You have brothers other than Caine?"

"I had six. Three of them died."

Silence hung over us. "I'm sorry."

The uneven dripping grew louder. My mind was still whirling, reviewing everything that had happened. Grand Master Savus striding out of the mist. Maddan throwing a fit, insisting—despite all evidence—that he'd actually killed more angels than I had.

"We'll get out of here," said Ruadan quietly.

"How?"

"I'm still working on that."

"Who do you think told Savus about Baleros?" I asked.

"Do you have any idea where Ciara is?" he asked abruptly.

"I have no idea." My heart began to race. "Do you think Savus has her? What if he tortured it out of her?"

"Shh…" he said. "Save your energy. Panicking won't help her."

I wanted to slam my fist into the wall. Of course panicking wouldn't help, but what else could I do at this point? My breath was coming in short, sharp bursts, and my heart raced wildly. I rested my head in my hands, gritting my teeth so I wouldn't sob or scream.

"Your breathing sounds panicked."

I didn't answer him. I was too focused on trying not to scream with rage. I leaned back against the wall, sucking in a sharp breath as the jagged rocks pierced the wounds on my back.

"You're in a lot of pain," he said. "Hold on."

His dark magic whispered around my skin, and spirals of shadows wrapped around me, sliding over my skin. I sighed as his calming magic stroked my body, until I couldn't feel the pain anymore. I ran my fingertips over the skin on my side. He'd completely healed it.

His magic continued to caress my skin, calming my nerves, until my eyes drifted closed. His magic started to ebb, and yet sleep was claiming my mind. Once more, I dreamt of Emain.

* * *

WHEN I WOKE, I couldn't feel his magic anymore.

"Ruadan?" I called out.

The only response was the uneven dripping of water.

Gods damn it. Had he gone unconscious, or had they dragged him out of the cell to kill him? I fought the urge to slam my fist into the wall. Breaking my hand wouldn't do any good.

Groaning, I stood in my cell. How long would Savus keep me in here? I gritted my teeth, my fingers twitching.

Ruadan had healed me, and with my body now strong, I felt an overwhelming urge to hurt the people who'd put us here. When I closed my eyes, I could envision myself punching Savus in the jaw, over and over, smashing that creepy grin off his face.

When I heard the murmuring of voices farther down the hall, and saw the flickering of warm light over the damp stone, my heart sped up. Footfalls moved closer over the stone.

Savus hadn't wanted to kill me, because it would put him at odds with the Old Gods. But he seemed to think he'd found a loophole by asking Ruadan to kill me. Let someone else take the fall for him. I imagined he hoped I'd simply start failing the trials, or perhaps that Maddan would properly kill me at some point. But Maddan was so amazingly incompetent that here I was, still alive. Ready to savage my enemies.

Still, I could now accept that there was no way Savus was allowing me into the Institute of the Shadow Fae. Old Gods or not, my invitation had been canceled.

As I stared through the bars, Maddan's smug face showed up outside my cell. He held a torch, and its warm light lit up his face from below, giving him a devilish look.

Ciara's voice rang in my mind. *The devil wears many faces.*

I imagined Maddan had been up in his room for days, dreaming of this moment in such a fevered state that he'd run out of tissues. Was he here to kill me?

"Arianna," he purred.

This time, it didn't look as if he'd brought any distilled magic with him.

My lip curled. "Maddan. You couldn't win the trials, so you've come here to kill me."

"No, I've just come to look at you in your filthy little cage." The bulge in his trousers confirmed my tissue theory. "Grand Master Savus won't let me kill you. It seems he has a plan for a public execution of you and Ruadan. I can't wait to see it."

"Why does he want us dead?"

He arched an eyebrow. "I'm not supposed to say."

I snorted. "As if you're privy to that information. There's no way he'd trust an incompetent idiot like you. You're just a pawn in all this. Not a real player."

"Bollocks." He spat. "I know plenty. You're leverage, just like Ruadan is."

I rolled my eyes dramatically. "Oh, sure. That makes sense." I prodded. "Leverage for what?"

"Baleros wants you dead. He wants both of you dead. He needs the World Key from Ruadan. You? I think he just hates you. Just like I do."

Rage slammed into me. I gripped the iron bars, ignoring the fact that they burned my skin, and I stared into Maddan's eyes. "Grand Master Savus is working with Baleros? Enemy of the Shadow Fae?"

So that's how Grand Master Savus knew about my connection to Baleros. Baleros had told him right out. Savus had been giving up my location all along, sending assassins to try to kill me during the trials. Why would they be working together—the leader of the Shadow Fae, and one of their greatest enemies? "Why?" I gritted out. "Why is Savus working with a traitor to the Shadow Fae?"

Maddan's mouth closed, his lips pressed into a thin line. It seemed he realized that he'd said too much.

"I'm not saying anything else. I'll see you again when it's time to kill you."

The world fell out from under my feet. I wasn't sure how I'd save Ruadan and myself, but I would. I wasn't going to let these creeps slaughter us.

Maddan cocked his head. "Do you know that I've always dreamed of having a little prisoner like you of my own? My father wouldn't let me have one. He says madness runs in our family line. And it does, you know. My grandfather's favorite courtier was his pet lion. He made him his Minister of Festivals. He used to feed the gutter fae to his lion, William. When I was a boy, I'd go to watch. I wanted some of the gutter fae slaves for my own." He closed his eyes, a smile curling his lips. "The females' clothes were often torn, just rags, so I could see their shameful parts."

I blinked. *Shameful parts?* "Can you go now? I prefer the sound of my own screaming in my mind."

"With your short little dress on, I can almost see your shameful parts."

"Oh my gods, *stop.*"

But he was still standing there. "Eventually, the gutter fae rose up and slaughtered my grandfather. My father became king. He had all sorts of ideas about keeping the gutter trash happy." He opened his eyes again, moving closer. "But I want one little gutter fae for my own. Just one." His cheeks were pink, his eyes glazed with fever. "Too bad you'll be dead soon. Still, I'll have the memory of you trapped in here."

My lips quirked in a smile. "Go on, then. Open this iron door. I'm right here for the taking."

If only I could get him to unlock the door, he'd be dead within moments…

He took a step back into the shadows. "I'm not that stupid. I'll have to admire you from here."

I closed my eyes, frustration rising. When I opened them again, he was gone.

CHAPTER 27

Without Ruadan's help, I could no longer sleep on my own. I crouched against the rough wall in the Palatial Room, trying to think about Emain. Sadly, it seemed that I couldn't summon the vivid visions myself.

My heart rate quickened at the sound of footfalls moving down the hallway again.

Savus held a torch in his silver hand, and the light danced over his crown. Soft and black like rotten banana peels, it hung limp over his skull.

I glared at him, envisioning myself killing him. If I could get myself out of here, perhaps I could rip off his silver arm and batter him half to death with it…

I flashed him a charming smile. "How nice to see you. Where the fuck is Ruadan? If you kill him, I swear to the gods I will find a way to rip every inch of flesh off your body."

"Arianna. You don't need to worry. He's still alive. For now. And I won't be exalting you. However, I will behead the both of you with an iron sword." He pursed his lips. "Or at least I'll have Maddan do it for me."

My body shook with rage. "You're working with Baleros. You've been giving him my location all along." I narrowed my eyes. "Were you throwing butterscotch sweets in my cell for him? Seriously, what the hells?"

He sighed. "Baleros has been giving us instructions. He did say the sweets would upset you, but he never explained why."

I still didn't understand. What was Savus getting out of this? "How can you betray the Institute this way?"

He stared at me. Along with his sagging crown, his shoulders looked slumped, no longer the rod-straight posture of a Grand Master.

He arched an eyebrow. "I suppose Maddan was the one who told you about this. He can't keep his mouth shut." His hand shook—a tremor I'd never seen before. Something had broken him. "But you're going to die anyway, so I suppose it doesn't matter what you know."

I felt as if a weight pressed on my chest. "Why do you want Ruadan and me dead?"

Grand Master Savus flinched. Then, he tapped a shaking, gloved hand against his silver fingertips, eying me through the bars.

"Why?" I shouted again.

"I don't. Killing you means I forfeit my crown and my power." Mist billowed around him. He clenched his hand into a fist, his jaw tightening with rage. "But Baleros demands it, doesn't he? He wants the World Key, of course. And he wants you dead. I have to comply with his demands." His voice cracked. "I tried to resist. I tried to find a way around it. I deserve to be the Grand Master. But I find I'm quite unable to resist his demands."

"Why?" I gritted out. "What leverage does he have on you?" Baleros always had leverage.

Savus cocked his head. "After you and Ruadan nearly

killed him in the arena, he sent me a message. It was the first time I'd heard from him in over a century. It seems he's been keeping a secret for fifteen years."

"Fifteen years." The time frame sounded familiar. "Fifteen years ago was when he invaded Emain. That's when he killed Queen Macha." As soon as the words were out of my mouth, I began putting the pieces together. Baleros would never be so stupid as to kill a queen. That wasn't his M.O. Sure, he could kill someone like me. He'd always been willing to sacrifice my life. No one important cared about me.

But a queen, on the other hand—what could he get for a queen? Baleros collected leverage years in advance of playing his hand. Just like he had with Ciara.

I stared at Savus. "Queen Macha isn't really dead, is she?" Ruadan had said that her body was unrecognizable.

His gaze clouded, shoulders slumping even more. "I thought she was. Until Baleros sent me one of her fingers, just after you went missing." His voice cracked. Now I was getting a hint of what had broken him. "I'd know it anywhere. The golden skin, the delicately tapered fingertips. The sheen on her nails. I was her loyal subject for centuries. I kissed the rings on those fingers, bent my knee. She was the greatest ruler Emain had ever known." He met my gaze, his eyes filled with pain. "Baleros has been keeping her hidden in an unknown location. Trapped by some sort of magic. I've been sending a few Shadow Fae on secretive missions to find her, but to no avail. I have had no choice," he said through gritted teeth.

My breath was coming in short, sharp bursts. "If Baleros has had the queen all along, why did he go through all the rigmarole of sending assassins into the Institute? Why not just—I don't know—get Ruadan to do his bidding, open up worlds in exchange for his mother's life?"

"He doesn't want to get anywhere near Ruadan, not

without dozens of iron arrows pointed at the Wraith's body. Baleros is terrified of him. He waited as long as he could to play his trump card. He tried getting his lackeys to steal the World Key. He tried getting you to steal it. He feels that he's now out of options. He's using the best bargaining chip he has. The fingers of a queen we all love." His eyes glistened. "I tried to resist. The Old Gods chose Ruadan, and they chose you. I couldn't send the mist army after you, or the Old Gods would steal my power. I hoped there was another way. I hoped you'd die in a trial, or fail one."

"You really thought Maddan could beat me?"

He shrugged. "No, not really, but it was a hope. And while I kept you here in prison, delaying his requests, Baleros bade me to do things to torment you. Butterscotch sweets, locking you in a cell… But he grew impatient when I failed to kill you. He wanted his World Key. I never wanted to kill Ruadan. She'll be so angry with me. But Baleros sent me another one of her beautiful fingers. You see that I had no choice, don't you? There was no other choice."

He had a hungry look, and I got the impression that he actually wanted my approval for his decisions. Like he wanted me to agree that executing Ruadan and me was clearly the best course of action.

I gritted my teeth. I wasn't giving him the redemption he was looking for. "And you have no idea where he's keeping her?"

"Do you honestly think that I wouldn't rescue her if I knew where she was?" he shouted, his voice bellowing off the stones. His eyes flashed. For a moment, intense fury contorted his features, and I had a vision of the formidable man he must have been at one time. Then, his eyes dulled again.

The way he described the queen's fingers made me think he was more than a loyal subject.

"You're in love with Queen Macha," I said. "That's why Baleros could manipulate you so easily."

Savus's mist whipped around him. "She was supposed to marry me. Centuries ago, she was supposed to be mine. But I couldn't marry her after she sullied herself with that incubus, and after she gave birth to Ruadan. He was a mistake that ruined both our lives."

"Of course, I understand. Ruadan's entire existence is a slap in your face, isn't it? A living symbol of your life's ruination." My lip curled. "Is it really all Baleros's doing, or do you just want to correct this blight on your life?"

The mist thickened around Savus. "I am doing what I must to protect a queen of Emain. That is all."

I could tell by the shaking of his hands that I'd rattled him.

"Do you honestly think Queen Macha could love you after you kill her son? You can't erase a mistake when the mistake is a person's child."

Savus's face turned pink. "I resisted Baleros's demands for as long as I could. But Baleros will rip her apart! He will exalt her!"

"You could turn the mist army against *him.*"

"The goddess of fire would simply revive him. He can't be killed."

"Everything can be killed," I snarled. "You really haven't tried. You're giving a monster like Baleros the power to control the portals? You really think that's a good idea? I don't think you understand. Queen Macha won't just be *angry*. She will *hate* you with every cell in her body. His mother will want you dead—"

He flicked his hand and mist slid over my mouth, solidifying into a gag. Furious, I screamed into it.

"You're right," he said. "I can't let her know that I gave the command." He tapped his fingertips together. "We'll do this in private. Maddan will strike the blows. He's been eager to do that. I'll blame it on him, then I'll have him killed as well. Queen Macha will be so pleased when I exalt him. I don't care if I anger his father. I'm willing to make that sacrifice. You see?" His eyes shone in the darkness, the terrifying gleam of a fanatic. "I am willing to make that sacrifice for my queen."

I shouted into my gag, my chest heaving.

He arched an eyebrow. "I know what you're thinking. It's a betrayal of the Institute. But the truth is, I'm making a sacrifice for the good of Emain." He tapped a finger against his lip, eying me warily. "You're dangerous. I'm going to need to subdue you."

He flicked his hand again, and the mist covered my nose so I couldn't breathe. As my lungs burned, I knew what he was doing. Smothering me, knocking me unconscious until I no longer posed the smallest of threats to him.

CHAPTER 28

I couldn't see much when I awoke—just the mist around me, and the contours of mist soldiers. A small cohort surrounded me, fog wafting off their silhouettes.

Even if I couldn't see much, I sure as shit could feel the iron garrote searing my throat. So *this* is where Baleros had learned about the iron garrote—apparently an Institute classic. Rope bound my wrists behind an iron stake, and the metal scalded my skin. My hands were crammed between the stake and a jagged stone wall.

The mist had been taken from my nose so I could breathe again, but it still gagged my mouth. A jagged edge of stone bit into my fingers, practically crushing them against the stake.

By the dim sound of dripping water and the heavy, mildewed feel of the air, I had the sense that we were in an underground space, one without open windows.

I'd tried to talk Savus out of a public execution. Instead, I'd given him the idea to secretly assassinate us.

"Arianna?" Ruadan's voice echoed off the stones.

I screamed into the damned mist gag, then I willed my heartbeat to slow, trying to think clearly.

As I surveyed the hall around me, I flexed my wrists. When I looked up, I could see the contours of the room. A high, mossy ceiling arched a hundred feet above us. No windows. It seemed to be an enormous underground hall, and iron torture devices hung from the stone above. Not a fitting place for the prince of Emain to die.

Then, torchlight tinged the mist with warm light, and footfalls clacked over the stone. From between the mist soldiers, Maddan stalked closer, a silver-hilted sword slung at his hip. I had no doubt the blade was iron, ready to dispatch us. My heart was a hunted animal.

I wanted to vomit into my gag. Frantically, I rotated my wrists back and forth to loosen the bindings. If I managed to free my hands—well, I'd still be shit out of luck, because iron pinned my neck to the stake. But with my hands free, maybe I could attack Maddan if he got close enough…or delay things until I thought of a better idea.

I grimaced, now shifting the ropes up and down against the jagged rock. Maybe I could saw through them.

Maddan bit his lip at the sight of me, his cheeks reddening. He stroked his fingertips over the silver hilt of his sword, up and down, up and down.

I shot a quick glance in the direction of Ruadan. As the mist shifted, I caught a glimpse of him. His arms were bound to a stake behind his spine, an iron garrote at his neck. All that iron around him would dampen his powers, sapping his strength.

Maddan unsheathed his sword, a smile curling his lips as he stared at me. "I'm glad you now understand the proper order of things." His gaze nervously slid to Ruadan, as if he were scared the incubus was about to break free and rip his head off.

"I never wanted to execute a prince," said Maddan. "It goes against everything I was raised to believe. But Grand Master Savus said that I had to. It's the only way I can become a Shadow Fae. The only way he'd let me slaughter the gutter trash. As you can see, I don't have a choice in this."

I glanced at Ruadan again. For once, no dark magic whipped around him, since the iron absorbed it all. He glared at Maddan, his eyes completely black. He didn't say a word, his animal stillness taking over. Was he just going to stand there, completely still, until the iron sword cut into his throat?

A grin spread on Maddan's face, as he seemed to forget Ruadan was in the room. He prowled closer to me, and my skin crawled.

Behind Maddan, the cohort of mist soldiers marched forward, armor glinting in the torchlight.

Panic started to crawl up my throat.

Maddan licked his lips. "I just want to savor this moment. A pretty little gutter fae, bound by iron." His voice was a groan. "All mine. I'll be thinking about this for a long time."

By the creepy-as-fuck leer on his face, I knew he'd forgotten about Ruadan altogether. I just focused on the small but rapid movements behind my back. *Up and down, up and down.*

Mist whirled around the room, snaking over the floor and curling around our bodies, rushing over the rough contours of the stone walls. I could hardly see the soldiers anymore—only Maddan in front of me. The mist was a mercy, concealing the subtle shake of my shoulders that might otherwise give away my attempt to saw through the rope.

Dimly, I could hear the faint, almost inaudible groan of metal coming from somewhere near Ruadan. What was he doing over there?

Maddan, the sick twat, looked all too thrilled with this situation. Maybe I could keep him distracted long enough to cut through the rope. I opened my eyes wide in a mimicry of terror and screamed into my gag.

Maddan groaned with pleasure. He couldn't possibly imagine that right now, I was thinking of how it would sound when the crack of his bone echoed off the stones.

Up and down, up and down.

I longed for anything to disrupt Savus's plans, to delay the point when the blade would hack into our throats…anything to give us time to figure a way out.

When Maddan clamped his hand on my waist, I nearly threw up. Instead, I distracted myself with images of his death. Let's see…an iron nail through the heart, one in his skull. *Up and down, up and down.*

The sword, of course, would be easiest—

At last, the final bit of rope snapped, and my hands burst free. I grabbed Maddan's head—one hand around the back, one on his jaw. I twisted, and the crack of bone sounded off the stone ceiling.

Maddan's body slumped to the ground with a dull thud, and I stared down at him, smiling under my gag.

Slowly, the fog began to part, and Savus stepped forward.

"You killed my executioner," he said. Then, a long sigh. "I suppose he's not fully dead. Until he recovers, I'll have to find another." He tutted. "Honestly. This is highly inconvenient."

Truthfully, I'd hoped for a bit more of a reaction than that.

Still, that faint, nearly imperceptible groan of metal… what *was* that?

Savus flicked his wrist, and the mist snaked around my hands, binding them from the front. Sadly, this was a binding I wouldn't be able to saw off.

Savus crossed out of the room, his footsteps clapping

over the stone floor. But he'd left his soldiers behind to watch us, and their silver eyes burned through the fog.

* * *

I'M NOT sure how much time had passed by the time Savus returned with his new executioner. Pinned to an iron stake by a garrote that burned my throat, I was running on cage time. It had seemed like four hours, so it was probably about twenty minutes. Twenty minutes of silence broken only by the faint, nearly inaudible sound of groaning metal.

A new figure stalked into the room, dressed in a black cloak, a cowl over his head. He gripped an iron sword.

It took me a moment to realize the hands were not a man's, but were delicate, with a rich bronze color.

My heart galloped. *Melusine* was going to kill us? She wouldn't.

"They are enemies of the Institute," Savus's voice boomed off the damp stone walls. "Traitors working with one of our greatest enemies. I have reported them to the High Council of Emain, and we have received permission to execute. They are agents of Baleros. They are an insidious infection that will destroy the Institute from within…I have allowed them to live, and my crown has withered. We must correct this at once."

Melusine pulled down her cowl. She stepped closer, the mist coiling around her face. "Honestly, Grand Master Savus, I'm a little perplexed. Why do you want me to kill them?"

His low growl boomed through my gut. "As I said, they are enemies of the Institute. Traitors. If you do as you are asked, you will be inducted as one of the Shadow Fae. You will have proven yourself, and you can take Ruadan's spot. I know that's what you've always wanted—to be a Shadow Fae. Now, you'll no longer have to return home in disgrace. Isn't that what you want, Melusine? To be a hero? For your life to mean something? I know it was lonely for you back home. This is your chance. It's a matter of good and evil, as I'm sure you understand."

His voice had a soothing quality that snaked over my skin, almost convincing me that this was all a perfectly logical state of affairs. *Of course it made sense that we should die.*

Maddan shifted at my feet, gasping for breath, but his eyes hadn't yet opened. He groaned. When he awoke, he'd hack our heads off within moments. Even an idiot like him would know better than to screw around a second time.

Savus didn't want Queen Macha to know that he'd given the order. If I had to guess, his plan probably involved slaughtering Melusine right after she dispatched us.

I glanced at Ruadan, hoping to see a sign that he had a plan, that he was working on something, but he was completely still. Had he simply accepted his fate? He seemed like the kind who would try to go out with dignity or something asinine like that. I'd go out screaming and clawing at flesh, bellowing curses into the void.

Melusine wrinkled her nose, staring at me. "Thing I don't get, Grand Master Savus, is why you came to get me and handed me this sword. Seems to me like you don't want to kill them yourself. Seems like you don't want your mist soldiers to kill them, either. I see Maddan here, lying on the floor, and that looks like a failed attempt at an execution to me. Then you come get me, try to get me to do it. I put two and two together. I may not be the strongest, but my intellectual capacities are fully intact. I can do six kinds of math. And what I see here is that you're looking for a loophole, trying not to anger the Old Gods by getting someone else to do your dirty work. Now—"

"Kill them!" Savus's voice boomed. "Or I'll turn the mist soldiers on you. You ungrateful wretch. I'll have them tear you limb from limb, and boil your flesh in heated iron. The Old Gods don't protect you."

Her face blanched as the mist soldiers began moving closer to her. Still gripping the iron sword, she held up her hands. "Now hang on. Hang on. Let's just think this through."

On the ground, Maddan shifted again, groaning.

The mist soldiers took another step closer to Melusine. Through the swirls of fog, I couldn't see the expression on her face, but when she spoke again, I could hear the tremor in her voice. "I'm just asking that we all think—"

Maddan leapt to his feet, and he snatched the sword from Melusine. He whirled, turning on me. As he moved closer through the fog, I could see the fury etched on his features.

Then, a loud groan of creaking metal. My gaze flicked to Ruadan. Through the mist, I could barely make out what he was doing. He was pulling the garrote apart with his bare hands. Even with all the iron around him, weakening his body, he was powerful enough to *bend* the metal. Never underestimate a demigod, apparently.

Joy bloomed in my heart at the sight of his garrote separating from the stake.

Maddan raised the sword, ready for a swing, and panic paused my heart for just a moment.

Then, the rumbling of the ground beneath us stopped Maddan's swing—an earthquake that shook through my bones.

CHAPTER 29

"What's going on?" Maddan shrieked, trying to keep his balance.

Stone began crumbling beneath my feet, the floor cracking. Through the cracks, I caught a glimpse of dark, churning waters, flecked with stars. Ruadan was opening a portal.

While Savus and Maddan shouted for the mist soldiers to attack, the world fell away under my feet, and I plunged into icy water.

As I sank deeper under the water, hot wrath simmered inside me. Someday, I'd quench my fury with blood. I wanted to kill Savus, Maddan, all of them…

In the cold waters, the mist around my arms and mouth began to dissolve. Unfortunately, I was still trapped to the damn stake by the iron garrote. Worse, the stake was connected to a large chunk of stone, and the whole thing was pulling me in deeper underwater, choking me as I sank into the portal. I flailed around, kicking in the water, but I couldn't move myself upwards. My lungs were on fire.

At last, a powerful arm looped around my waist.

I held my breath, sinking underwater, and I stared into

Ruadan's violet eyes. Already, the presence of his magic and his body's warmth soothed me.

He reached for the garrote around my neck. Gritting his teeth, he pulled at it, bending the metal.

Nothing particularly clever, no magic. He was just unbelievably strong, even when the iron around him had dampened his powers.

Freed from the garrote, I kicked my legs, swimming for the surface. My lungs felt as if they might explode, but I stared with relief at the rays of light piercing the water. Hope began to bloom in my chest. Above us, I could see other bodies moving, kicking to the surface. Soldiers from the mist army must have fallen in. But as I swam, they began to dissolve in the icy water like sugar.

The iron sword—the one Maddan had been holding—drifted down, and I caught it by the hilt. Had Maddan fallen through as well? I hoped he had. I'd drive this weapon right through his throat.

Now, I saw only moon rays piercing the surface. If Maddan had pulled himself out of the water first, he'd probably be waiting for us at the portal's exit, ready to strike.

At last, I breached the surface. I gasped for breath, frantically scanning for signs of Maddan, but I saw only a dark orchard, and a starry sky arching high above us. I still gripped the sword. As I caught my breath, it took me a few moments to recognize that we'd emerged in a fountain. Unlike the fountain in Lilinor, this one looked natural—a small geyser spurting out of a rough, stone-rimmed pool. Water rained down from above.

I sucked in air to fill my lungs, and grasped onto the lip of the fountain. When I glanced behind me, I saw Ruadan climbing out of the water on the other side of the fountain.

Still gripping the sword, I followed suit. Exhausted, I flopped down on the wet soil. By the heavy scent of apples in the air—a smell that Ruadan carried with him—I had the sense that he'd brought us to Emain. But that wasn't my most pressing issue right now. I pushed myself up again, surveying the space around us.

First things first. Establish the existence of a threat.

"I think Maddan came through." I lifted the sword, still catching my breath. "Found this sinking in the water."

Ruadan sniffed the air. "I think you're right. But he was wearing the lumen stone. He must have leapt away from us."

"You don't sense him around us?"

"No, but we'll need to find him."

I inwardly cursed myself for my sluggishness, relative to Ruadan. If I hadn't been here, he could have shadow-leapt after Maddan. Instead, Ruadan was waiting for me.

"Bloody right we need to find him," I grumbled. "Let me have the honor of severing his head, please."

Ruadan's magic snaked over my skin, raising goosebumps. "Not yet. We need to capture Maddan as soon as we can and take him to Emain's High Council."

"Why?" I asked.

"Emain's High Council is the central seat of Shadow Fae power. We need their permission to execute Grand Master Savus. Without their approval, all the world's Shadow Fae will hunt us down."

"And why do we need Maddan for permission to kill Savus?" My wet black dress stuck to my body, and I hugged myself. I was still shaking from my brush with death. Disoriented, I struggled to focus.

Ruadan rubbed the back of his neck. "He'll be the evidence we'll submit at the trial. He's our witness."

At this point, it occurred to me that Ruadan still didn't know the truth behind what had just happened. With all the drama of being knocked unconscious and nearly executed, it had slipped my mind a bit. Ruadan still didn't know *why* Grand Master Savus was doing all this.

"Let's go," said Ruadan. "I've scented Maddan's path."

"Wait! There's something you should know."

Ruadan whirled, his shadows whipping around him.

I stared at him, at a loss for words. I wasn't great with tact, but this would pose a conundrum even for the most diplomatic and empathic of people. How did you tell someone that his mother wasn't actually dead, but his worst enemy had been holding her for years?

"Well, there's good news and there's bad news," I began. "I'll just get right to the point. I won't dance around it. At least, I think it's good news and bad news, according to Grand Master Savus. If he can be trusted. Can he be trusted? The point is, I'll just say it. Of course, he can't be trusted, though, he just tried to sever our heads…so, taking that with a grain of salt—"

Ruadan raised a hand. "Stop. What are you trying to tell me?"

I took a deep breath, marshaling a sense of calm. "Just before Grand Master Savus knocked me unconscious and dragged me to the execution chamber, we had a little chat. He claims that Baleros never really killed your mum, and that he's been holding her as a pawn for fifteen years. Waiting for a moment to use her. Grand Master Savus is in love with her, so he was doing Baleros's bidding by trying to kill us both in exchange for the queen."

Ruadan went completely still, his eyes dark as the night sky. A gust of wind toyed with his pale hair. At the sight of him—so predatory and still—a shudder crawled over my skin.

Might as well tell him everything, though.

"Savus said that Baleros sent two of your mother's fingers," I went on. "The Grand Master recognized them.

That's why he was so desperate to act. He thought that getting others to kill for him was a loophole or something idiotic."

Near silence greeted me, just the sound of the wind rustling the trees, and crickets chirping in the distance.

"Maddan was in on it, too," I added. I wanted to make sure Ruadan hated him as much as I did, so that when we killed him, it would really hurt.

Ruadan's magic billowed so deeply around him, it looked like a blanket of darkness. The temperature dropped about twenty degrees, and my wet dress felt like it was going to freeze to my body. The air misted in front of my face as I breathed in and out.

"Could you stop with the ice?" I asked. Then, feeling tactless, I added. "Sorry about your mum. I mean, the fingers. Good that she might be alive, though, right?"

If one of our trials had involved tact, the Old Gods would have turned on me in seconds. I'd never have made it this far.

Then, switching to a more comfortable line of conversation, I added, "We will hunt down everyone who hurt her and rip their spines from their bodies, starting with Baleros. Even if the fire goddess revives him, we can still brutally punish him while he lives. Furthermore, I will beat Savus to death with his own silver arm." There. That was my best attempt at being comforting.

My teeth chattered, and some of the ice receded from the air.

At last, Ruadan spoke. "Where is she?"

"Savus said he doesn't know. He sent some Shadow Fae looking for her, and I expect he killed them, too, because he didn't want this secret getting out. After he told me, he sealed my mouth and prepared to have me executed. But we'll find her. I promise."

Shadows seeped into the air around Ruadan. "Savus has hated me for years."

"Right. I don't think it's because your mum died. I think it's because he's in love with her."

He nodded once, almost imperceptibly. "I see. He resents me."

I inhaled sharply, crossing closer to Ruadan. I stood so close to him that I could feel the heat radiating off his body. "He wanted you dead."

Ruadan's magic pulsed around him, floating on the breeze and seeping into the forest. His body was still as stone while the breeze whipped at his hair. At last, he spoke. "The plan remains essentially the same. We get permission to depose Grand Master Savus. We find out what he really knows through an interrogation. Then, we kill him. After he dies, we go after Baleros, and my mother."

"You still want to find Maddan?"

Ruadan nodded. "We will need him, yes. Grand Master Savus has reported us to the High Council as traitors. They won't take our word alone."

I shivered in the cold air, teeth chattering, until Ruadan pulled me tight against him. His body warmed mine until my teeth stopped chattering, and my muscles relaxed.

"Keep your eyes alert as we move through the forest," he said. "Rivers and streams run all around us. Here, the forest is full of fae who can lure you into insanity. There are gancanagh, who will seduce you until you lose your mind, and bean nighe, who will drag you under the water to your death. Fuathan live in the waters, protecting this realm from invaders. There are birdlike creatures, spirits of the unquiet dead who will swoop down and drive you insane. All are here to protect Emain from invaders. Sentinels of a sort."

"So we need to try to find out where Maddan went, before one of these monsters slaughters him. Maybe you should shadow-leap after him. He's not exactly the sort who would live long in any kind of dangerous situation."

"I'm not leaving you on your own."

I gripped the sword tighter. "You really think I can't handle the fae sentinels here?"

"I know you can fight them, but they're not ordinary opponents. The forests can be confusing, and they can muddle your mind. They can lead you astray."

"The sentinels wouldn't come after you, would they? You're not an invader."

"I am now. I've been away a long time. Just remember, Arianna. Here, things are not always as they seem."

CHAPTER 30

We walked through the forest, and I moved as quickly as I could, trying to keep up with Ruadan. He didn't speak, but my pace must have frustrated him. I moved faster than an ordinary fae, but I couldn't shadow-leap.

We sniffed the air as we traveled, following Maddan's path. Given what I knew about him, he'd probably arrived in Emain, panicked, then blindly run off in a random direction with literally no plan.

As we walked, the apple orchards gave way to a thicker forest—oaks, elders, and rowans. Their boughs framed the starry night sky above us.

"Any idea where we're headed?" I asked after a while.

"Maddan doesn't know his way around Emain. It's an island, with a few cities on the eastern shore. The rest is wilderness, inhabited only by the most ancient fae. Fae so old they're practically part of the landscape. That's where he's heading."

"Have you ever been here before?"

"As part of the Shadow Fae training, we spent years out

here. And my mother used to take me here. She's the one who taught me to track and to hunt."

Once again, I had the impression that his mum sounded brilliant. I wanted to say something reassuring, something like, "She sounds like the kind of woman who would be fine in captivity," but everything I could think of sounded flippant and callous instead of reassuring. And what did I know? Maybe someone like Ruadan, who'd spent years training in the wild, didn't need reassurance.

"What were your parents?" Ruadan said, abruptly.

It was sort of a strange way to phrase a question. Not "*who* were your parents." He wanted to know what my other half was.

"Your guess is as good as mine." I hated lying. I wasn't even a good liar. Still, I couldn't tell him the truth.

I wanted to change the subject before he could ask for more details. Details like, "Where did you come from? When did you last see your parents?" Things I wanted to avoid.

"You said that Grand Master Savus hated you for years," I said. "What did he do to you?"

As soon as I felt the air frost around me, saw the breath misting in front of my face, I knew that I'd struck a nerve of some kind. At least I'd succeeded in changing the subject. A rough gust of wind slid over us, and I silently cursed the cold.

After a minute, I was certain he didn't want to answer.

Then, he shot me a quick look, his eyes shining in the darkness. "You've seen the tattoo on my back?"

"Yes. The fae word? What does it mean?"

"The Shadow Fae of Emain are divided into cohorts, each named after a type of tree. My cohort was the Yew. I had two half-brothers in the cohort—my mother's sons. We were together for centuries, training in Emain, fighting and assassinating enemies of our realm."

Already a sense of dread was curling around my ribs. He'd said that his brothers had died.

"When I joined the London Institute," he went on, "Grand Master Savus sent me on a mission. He told me to employ my old cohort—we were called the Eburones. Men of the Yew. Grand Master Savus told us we were hunting down an angel, someone who never should have come to Earth."

My mouth went dry. "What happened?" With an iron nerve, I willed my voice to remain steady.

"I had to open a portal to another world. The angel was hidden there, living with his family. They lived as part of a little village, in fact. It confused me when I arrived and spotted the cottage—a wife with red hair. And a son. A young boy who ran away as soon as we arrived. I didn't understand. Angels can't have children. The pleasure they'd feel when siring a child would cause them to fall."

I could hardly breathe as he spoke. All the air had left my lungs.

"It wasn't an angel," he went on. "Not an ordinary one. It was the Horseman of Death. One of the architects of the apocalypse. Do you know what sort of destruction such a creature can wreak?"

My mind went numb. Oh yes. I knew. "What happened to your cohort?" I asked in a remarkably steady voice, but I already knew the answer.

"Dead. Every single one of them died before my eyes."

I exhaled slowly. "Why didn't you die?"

"I was the only one there with the blood of a demon-god. I'm nearly impossible to kill. Unfortunately, Death can't be killed either. But after what he did, he is on my list, and I will figure out a way to end him and his line. He killed almost everyone I loved. He was protecting his son, but he hit his wife in the crossfire. I remember seeing her lying in the dirt.

He killed the other fae, too. The ones living with him. His son was the only one to get away."

My thoughts were racing out of control, and I willed my heartbeat to slow down. Ruadan could probably hear it. It would alert him that something was wrong. Only once I mastered control of myself did I speak again. "You want to kill his son?"

"Of course. Such a creature is monstrous. He'd be a grown man now. I just need to learn who he is."

My blood roared in my ears. "And Savus is the one who sent you on that mission."

"Yes. A part of me always wondered if he'd done it on purpose. Perhaps it hadn't just been a mistake. But maybe he'd known that Death lurked there.

A heavy silence fell over us. "I'm sorry you lost your cohort," I said at last. "And your half-brothers. Do you have any family left?"

"No. My younger sister inherited the throne, but that was it."

"If she's younger, why didn't you inherit the throne?" I asked. "Or what about Caine?"

"Bastard."

"Beg your pardon?"

"I was illegitimate. And Caine and I are related on my father's side. The city's elders debated the line of succession, but in the end, they chose Queen Brigantia. Fine with me. I'm more of a warrior than a prince."

"Your own sister won't believe you without proof?"

"She will, I think. But the High Council will not."

My mind still whirled back to everything Ruadan had told me earlier—the attack on the horseman, his entire cohort dying.

My skull roiled with images of dead fae, littering a field. I could almost smell the death…but just as soon as the scent of decay filled my nose, it dissipated, and I breathed in the smell of fresh bread. It reminded me of home. Home before Baleros had found me. Where raspberries grew all around us.

Now, the light seemed to grow brighter—shining silver moonlight that gleamed through the trees. As I walked, I could no longer see Ruadan, but it didn't bother me. I felt at peace.

A flicker of movement through the dark bushes caught my attention, and a new scent filled the air. The briny scent of the ocean. I closed my eyes, breathing it in. I licked my lips, tasting salt. Night cloaked my body like silk.

When I opened my eyes again, a handsome man was standing before me in the dark grove. His long, brown hair fell over his shoulders. He had full eyebrows, a neatly trimmed beard, and his clothing looked as if it had been made from the colors of the forest itself: rich greens and browns, a velvety texture. Pale smoke curled from an ivory pipe in his lips.

"Welcome," he said. He spoke in Ancient Fae—a language I'd never learned. And yet somehow, I could understand him. He stepped closer to me, his movements oddly silent. "Who walks before me with all the darkness and beauty of a cloudless, starry sky?" He took another step closer, and with a delicate stroke of his fingertip, he brushed a lock of my hair off my cheek. I shuddered at his touch.

"Your beauty is like the ocean," he purred, "stirring within me terror and ecstasy, an inexorable lure." His voice wrapped itself around my body, and I closed my eyes.

I hardly noticed myself dropping the sword to the soil. What did I need a sword for? Love was all around me.

"I will bathe you in morning dew." His fingertips were on my hips, stroking them in circles.

Where was I? I had no idea, and it didn't matter because nothing in the world mattered but the feel of his fingertips on my skin. Why was I wearing this stupid dress? The fae lived in nature. We weren't made to wear clothing.

As if hearing my thoughts, my new friend began inching up my dress. My skin started to heat.

I had a vague sense that I should be fighting him, that he was dangerous, but I couldn't bring myself to do it.

"When I'm around you," he went on, his honeyed voice licking at my skin, "a fevered heat blooms in me."

He pulled my dress off, and the heavy night wrapped itself around my bare skin. With an ecstatic shiver, I leaned back into his body. Hunger grew within me.

He stroked a hand down my skin, and my mind blazed with images of Ruadan—his golden skin, his powerful arms...

"Your breasts draw me in like the moon in Earth's orbit, the waves of your hair frame your face like the ocean frames the shore, and light radiates from your eyes—two perfect orbs like two moons."

This time, my body tensed at his voice. Was it just me, or was he a little bit of a knob? At this point, his metaphors were just confusing me, and he had at least three moons in that one.

Smoke curled from his white pipe, but I smelled something different in it. The scent of decay.

I pulled away from him, narrowing my eyes. Now, he looked a little different. The pipe he smoked looked like a human rib, and a drop of blood shone at the corner of his lips.

I took a step back from him. What had happened to Ruadan? And where was my dress? So *this* was the gancanagh. Honestly, I'd expected better game than this from a legendary seducer. This guy sucked.

He reached for me, his dark eyes wide. Now, his cheekbones looked sharp, his features a little too hungry. "A wild storm rages within my breast, a ruthless tempest. You are Diana, and I am—"

"Fuck off." I scanned the ground, searching for my dress, my sword. As I reached for the iron, the gancanagh lunged for me, canines bared. His teeth sank into my neck, and he yanked down my bra as he bit me.

Just moments ago, I'd wanted his hands all over me. Now, I yearned for the feel of knuckles hammering bone. I reared back my arm and slammed my fist into his face, over and over. My knuckles sang as I broke the skin on his skull, and it felt glorious.

Blood streamed from my throat where he'd bitten me, but I ignored it, focusing instead on pounding his face.

He grabbed my throat, fingers tightening. From below, I brought my elbow up into his jaw, knocking him off. He staggered back, and I punched him hard in the throat.

Something glinted out of the corner of my eye—the dull gleam of an iron blade. I grabbed the silver hilt, and the gancanagh reached for one of my legs. Surprisingly strong, he yanked me to the ground, and I slammed down hard on my back. The sword fell from my fingers, and the gancanagh's hands were around my throat again, squeezing until I thought my larynx might crush my spine. My eyes bulged, and the creature leaned down, groaning as he licked my cheek.

I grabbed one of his wrists, then rotated my hips until I managed to knock him off. I rolled, shifting him off me. I pinned him to the ground with my knee over his throat.

I punched him—once, twice—until his eyes looked glazed. Then, I shifted off him to snatch my sword from the earth.

As he rose to lunge for me, I swung the sword through his neck. Blood sprayed all over my bare skin, and his head rolled over the forest floor. With the fight finished, my pulse began to slow.

I looked down at myself. No bra or dress, covered in blood. I'm not sure I'd make a super convincing defendant when I showed up at the High Council to plead our case.

As I caught my breath, I spotted my black dress on the ground. I grabbed it. Grimacing, I used it to clean off the gancanagh's blood, leaving behind only a few streaks of red. With the cotton soaked in blood, I didn't want to put the dress back on. Instead, I crumpled it up and threw it next to the headless fae.

I'd have to ask for Ruadan's shirt.

Speaking of Ruadan, where the hells was he? The bastard thought he was going to protect me, and here I was getting attacked by creepy poets lurking in the bushes.

It took me a few moments to get my bearings, until I glimpsed the broken branches that marked my path back to the main trail. I pushed through the undergrowth, sticks scratching at my bare skin, until I found my way to the larger, clear path. I was wearing nothing but my knickers, but I held my hand over my breasts as I walked.

On the main path, I found not a single incubus. I considered yelling out for Ruadan, but decided I may not want to call any more attention to myself, particularly considering I was basically naked and reeking of ancient fae blood.

An alluring song floated through the tree boughs—a female voice. I sniffed the air, breathing in the scent of pine, a faint hint of apples. Ruadan was nearby. I spotted a few broken branches in the shrubs, and I sniffed the air again.

Well, well, well. Seems Ruadan got a bit distracted as well.

I cupped my breasts as I walked through the darkened forest, my feet crunching over the leaves, until the little path opened into a clearing. A sensual song floated through the night air, trembling over my skin. A sapphire pond glittered in the starlight, so beautiful I nearly missed the people standing by the lake's edge.

My chest tightened with irritation at the sight of Ruadan. Sirens dressed in sheer, gossamer dresses surrounded him, singing into his ears. Their wild berry-colored hair cascaded over delicate shoulders. The women—with very visible nipples—gripped his limbs, sliding their hands over his body. Pearly wings swooped down their backs, rhythmically beating the air.

Ruadan's eyes had turned black as the night sky, and he didn't seem to see me. The sirens' music lured me closer, their song a powerful tug in my chest.

I gripped the sword tighter. I ran my fingertips over the iron, using the pain to keep control of myself, even as the song seduced me. Ruadan's muscles tensed. With a grunt, he ripped himself away from the sirens. He whirled on them, snarling, canines bared. His dark magic poisoned the air, and the lake began to ice over. *Finally.*

The sirens' wings fluttered, feathers flying around as they scrambled away from him. Their beautiful song fragmented, the melodies falling apart. Then, they clambered back into the icy lake.

"Enjoying yourself, Ruadan?"

CHAPTER 31

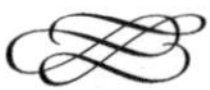

His head snapped toward me, eyes dark as pitch. "I was just leaving." His eyes slowly raked up and down my body. "Perhaps I could ask the same of you. It seems someone has divested you of your clothing."

"He's dead now. But it just seems like you were making a few friends."

His magic lashed the air around him as he stared at me. He went completely still, and I had the odd sensation that he was about to pounce on me like a wild animal.

After a moment of silence, he said. "You're wearing nothing but a few streaks of fae blood."

"Why are we still talking about that?" I snapped.

I crossed to the sirens, my eye on one with blue hair. Before she could escape me, I leaned down and gripped her arm *hard.* I pointed my sword at her. Chunks of ice floated around her, and her breath clouded the air. She blinked at me, pouting, her face a mask of innocence. I tried to ignore the fact that I'd now totally uncovered my breasts.

"I'm going to need your dress," I said. "Now."

She opened her mouth to sing, and my back started

arching at the sound. "Stop it!" I yelled. "I will sing over you. And nobody wants that. It's not pretty. Also, in case I wasn't clear, this sword is made of iron and I will cut out your larynx."

Did I feel bad for stealing a woman's dress at swordpoint? Maybe a little, but I *really* needed it, and I'm sure she could find a new one.

She pouted for a moment, then held out her free arm. The other sirens swarmed around her, untying the ribbons from her arms and back. They peeled off the gossamer fabric, and her breasts bobbed in the water. She scowled at me as she handed me the dress.

I let go of her arm as I snatched the dress from her, and the sirens began humming again.

I shot Ruadan a sharp look, clutching the gossamer fabric to the front of my body. "Let's get away from them before they start singing again."

"I was just leaving them."

"Were you now? Looked like you were standing there while they rubbed their gossamer tits all over you."

After a long silence, he said, "There were five of them." Then, his gaze slid over my body again. "You haven't explained what happened to your clothing."

"I met the gancanagh."

"And he stole your dress." I heard a hint of snarl in his voice.

"Yes. Before I killed him. He talked a lot. You know what I like?"

He didn't respond, but I answered anyway. "Men who don't talk too much."

For just a moment, the corner of his lips twitched in a smile. "I'll take the sword while you put the dress on."

He took the sword from me and turned away. With his back to me, I slipped the dress on. It was a bizarre cut, with holes in the back and swaths of fabric meant to accommodate wings. A series of ribbons hung down the back.

Freezing lake water soaked the dress. With the sheer fabric, it didn't hide much, and I'm not sure it was worth the bother.

"Ruadan? Can you tie up the back?"

He didn't say a word, but within moments, I felt his fingers nimbly moving up my spine as he tied the ribbons.

I turned to face him, and I held my hand out for the sword. But he wasn't handing it to me. Instead, his eyes were on my body. I watched them shift from violet to the darkness of night, and his magic snaked over my body.

In the sheer dress, and without my sword, I felt strangely vulnerable under his dark gaze.

"Ruadan," I said. "We need to find Maddan."

His eyes cleared again. "I know."

He crossed to me and handed me the sword.

"I'm amazed Maddan didn't get pulled in by the siren women," I said. "Apparently, he has better self-control than you. But honestly, Ruadan, it's a good thing you were around to save me, just like you said."

"I was about to leave them," he reiterated, a hint of a growl in his voice.

I sniffed the air. "There. Do you smell him? We're still on the right track."

Ruadan's eyes were on the ground. He didn't say anything, but after a moment, I caught what he was looking at—footprints, about the right size for Maddan. Gripping the sword, I crossed onto the main path. I moved as quietly as I could through the underbrush.

After a few minutes, the trail cut into the thicker forest. Here, broken branches and footprints signaled Maddan's route. Here, too, his scent grew stronger.

The distant sound of chatter pricked up my ears, until we reached a clearing.

As soon as we did, hunger gripped my stomach. Silver moonlight washed over a long banquet table laden with the most elaborate feast I'd ever seen: fruit pies, roast pheasant, bowls of strawberries, an entire duck, bread, and butter. My mouth watered.

I nearly missed the sight of Maddan. He was rolling around in the dirt in only his underwear, his pale skin covered in cream and smeared berries. His face beamed ecstatically.

"What's going on?" I asked.

Ruadan held a finger to his lips, then quietly whispered, "The enchantment of the forest has lured him in. But it's likely to be a trap."

I'd never seen his bare feet before, but now that I could, I realized they were comically small. Practically the size of a child's feet.

My nose wrinkled in disgust. No wonder he had that weird, lumbering walk.

I was about to take another step closer, when Ruadan grabbed me by the waist. My muscles tensed.

This didn't seem like a particularly dangerous situation—apart from the enduring psychological horror of watching Maddan roll around in cream and mashed berries. But of course, here, things were not always as they seemed. If this was a trap, it was like a fae spider's web. But what sort of fae sentinel was trapping us?

The shrill cry of a bird pierced the canopy of trees, and I looked up through the boughs, catching the silhouette of a crow against the moon.

When I looked back at the table, one of the pies was shaking and trembling, the crust bulging. A sharp beak pierced its surface, and a black bird burst from it. In the air, the bird transformed into a warrior, clad in black. Her white-blond hair whipped around her head, and she drew a sword—an iron blade, just like mine. She was enormous, practically the same size as Ruadan, and the sight of her sent a jolt of dread through my chest. The iron spikes jutting from her black leather didn't really lessen the intimidation factor. Here I was, in a gossamer-lake-water dress.

Ruadan leaned in, whispering in my ear. "Do you have this?"

"Yes." Already, battle fury raced through my limbs, making my legs shake.

Without waiting, I rushed for her, and our swords clashed. Within moments, we were whirling around each other, iron hammering against iron.

Through the clanging of our swords, I heard more birds dive for us, screeching. Ruadan was unarmed, but I wasn't too worried about him.

My opponent thrust her sword at me, but she left herself open on the right side. I drove my blade between her ribs.

She fell to the earth, and I whirled to take on the other attackers—three of them. For just a moment, I stared at Ruadan, who was fighting bare-handed. He was a maelstrom of fury, a whorl of black shadows and canines tearing into flesh. He was managing to fend off three attackers at once.

I cocked my head, learning from him as he fought. With his speed, no one could get a blow in. I liked watching him fight, and I stared as he snapped a warrior's neck. Shadows whipped through the air, and he whirled again. I smiled at the sound of crunching bone when he slammed his fist into a warrior's face.

Maddan was still rolling around on the ground, oblivious to the violence around him. Before he got the chance to clear his mind, I reached down and snatched the lumen crystal off his throat. I clasped it around my neck, and shadow magic rushed through my limbs. After a dizzying moment, I managed to evenly channel it throughout my body.

I gripped the sword again, but when I turned back to Ruadan, it was clear he didn't need my help.

In another five seconds, all three warriors were lying on the earth. They weren't dead, but they wouldn't be getting up in the next few minutes. Good enough.

Maddan pushed himself up onto his elbows, blinking. When his gaze landed on Ruadan and me, his face paled. He scrambled to his feet, reaching for the lumen crystal around his neck. It took him a moment to realize he'd lost it.

"Maddan," I said. "How lovely to see you again. I love the new look. Seems like you're doing fantastic since we last met. When was that? Oh, that's right, it was just an hour or so ago when you were about to slice off my head with this iron sword." I lifted it.

Ruadan stepped closer—two fae princes squaring off, one of them considerably more intimidating then the other.

"You're coming with us." Venom laced Ruadan's voice.

"You can't kill me," he sputtered. "My father will send an entire army after you. Grand Master Savus will, too."

"You're coming with us to the High Council," Ruadan interrupted him. "Put your clothes on."

I frowned at his feet. "Do you wear extra-large shoes to hide the ridiculous size of your feet? How do you even manage to stand?"

His face reddened, and he fell silent. Without another word, he snatched his clothing off the ground, frantically dressing himself. He was shaking so much, he didn't bother trying to clean the cream off his body. "Where are you taking me?" he asked.

"The High Council of Emain."

Maddan blinked, pausing with his trousers halfway up his legs. "Emain? Why are we going to see the High Council?"

I swung the iron sword in the air, carving it in sharp arcs before lowering it again. I just wanted to remind him that we could easily kill him. "All we need is for you to tell them what happened. Tell them what Grand Master Savus asked of you, and that Baleros has the queen."

"That's it?"

The ground trembled beneath our feet, and cracks of water opened within the soil.

It took me a moment to realize what was happening, and that magical light glowed from around Ruadan's body.

The ground gave way to icy water, and I plunged down beneath the depths, still gripping the sword. I held my breath as the water enveloped me.

The prince of Emain was *really* starting to piss me off with his lack of warnings.

CHAPTER 32

The jolt of freezing water shocked me. As I sank deeper, a few thoughts whirled in my mind. One, apparently you could take a portal within worlds, and not just between them. And two, I owed Ruadan the shock of an ice water bath as he slept.

At last, pale light streamed onto the water's surface from above, and I kicked my legs hard, swimming past Maddan. The silver orb of the moon appeared, and my hand pierced the surface. Still clinging onto the iron sword, I looped one arm over the stone lip of the portal's edge, and I hoisted myself out, gasping.

Ruadan had already climbed out, and he stood, his body dripping with water. He was staring up at the castle that loomed above us.

I clambered out of the water onto soil. "A little warning would be nice," I grumbled.

But my attention was already turning to the palace itself. A rocky, mountainous slope rose above us. The castle seemed to grow from the slope itself—its turrets made of uneven rock. Narrow gaps in the rocks formed windows—chinks of pale light in its walls. Thick ropes of tree roots and vines wound around the castle walls.

Inset into the base of the castle was an ornately carved wooden door.

The splashing and gasping behind me told me that Maddan had arrived through the portal.

Maddan sucked in breath so sharply he almost sounded like an animal. Then, he grasped for the fountain's rim. Grunting, he pulled himself over the edge and flopped onto the soil.

"How do we get in?" I asked.

Ruadan was already moving for the carved door. I grabbed Maddan by the arm, yanking him off the ground and dragging him toward the door. Still barefoot, he stumbled after me on his ridiculous small feet.

"Why do you need me to report to the High Council?" he protested. "Do you want me to explain to them that you're traitors who worked for Baleros?"

"They've already heard that story," I said through gritted teeth. "You need to tell them the part about how Grand Master Savus is working with Baleros."

"And what if I don't tell them that?" Maddan sniffed.

Ruadan whirled, and the look on his face, the darkness in his eyes, slid right through my bones. Despite his beauty, Ruadan's was a face from nightmares.

"In Emain, we interrogate people through torture. It's not reliable, but it's an old tradition. I could break your bones," said Ruadan, "one by one. It would delight me to hear your shrieks echo off the ceiling. Or, you could simply tell them the truth, like I've asked."

Maddan swallowed hard. "Torture? Even royalty from other realms?"

"We do things our own way here," said Ruadan. He whirled again, moving for the door. As we approached it, my eyes roamed over the carvings. It looked like it was made of oak, probably thirty feet high. A craftsman had carved it with pictures of stags, curling leaves, trees, and an engraved hand in the center.

When Ruadan reached it, he leaned down to his boot. He unsheathed a silver dagger. Then, he slid the blade across his palm, drawing blood. He pressed his bloodied palm against the engraved hand.

The door groaned, slowly sliding open, the weight of it shaking dirt from the rocky walls above us. Slowly, the enormous door heaved open.

"Is that an Emain royalty benefit?" I asked.

"The castle knows my blood."

The door rumbled open, revealing towering stone ceilings. Oak roots seemed to grow into stone around us, and torchlight faintly illuminated a vaulted ceiling that peaked hundreds of feet above us.

While I was gaping at the hall, Ruadan had already moved ahead, his footfalls echoing off the high arches.

I gripped Maddan's arm tighter, still dragging him along on his baby feet.

As we marched, a low, sonorous bell began to toll. An alarm, perhaps? Whatever it was, Ruadan didn't seem bothered, and he simply stalked onward.

At the end of the long hall, another set of wooden doors loomed over us. When Ruadan reached them, he pressed his hand against the door again. The doors groaned open over the stone floor.

In this hall, silver moonlight streamed through tall windows onto an ivory marble floor. An empty stony throne sat at one end of the hall.

I tightened my grip on the sword, with a chill rippling over my skin. How exactly had we been able to wander in here so easily? Ruadan was royalty with special door-opening blood, but we'd been reported as traitors. It was like this castle had no real defenses.

And yet as soon as the thought passed through my head, shadows whispered over the floor, whorls of smoke. Phantoms? The shadows spun faster, until they materialized into solid forms.

The sentinels wore black leather—all males. By their canines and pointed ears, I could tell they were fae as well as phantoms. But most importantly, they'd surrounded us, and they were thrusting swords at us. Maddan yelped behind me.

For a moment, I wondered if we were supposed to fight them. Since Ruadan never told me anything in advance, I had no idea.

"Lower your sword to the floor," Ruadan said quietly.

At last, he was filling me in.

Ruadan straightened, and when he spoke, his voice boomed over the hall. I had no idea what he was saying, since he'd launched into Ancient Fae. The only word I understood within the stream of sounds was "Ruadan," so I could only imagine he was announcing his entire lineage, possibly dating back to the Bronze Age. Seemed to be a bit of a thing for fae nobility.

The phantom-fae continued to stare at us, bodies unmoving. The silver in their eyes pierced the gloom of the hall. Their heads were cocked at unnatural angles. A draft whipped through the hall, lifting locks of their hair.

They crowded in closer around us, towering over us, until I could see nothing but the sentinels and their gleaming blades.

It felt freezing in the hall, and I was still wearing nothing but the waterlogged, gossamer gown. I regretted not getting the chance to strip the armor off the bird-warriors before Ruadan had ripped the ground out from underneath us.

It seemed like ages before the sound of heels clacked over

the hall, a staccato slap punctuating the air like gunshots. When silence descended, the phantom-guards fell away, still pointing their swords at us.

There, on the throne of rock, sat a woman in a sheer black gown that plunged to her navel. She crossed her long legs, and platinum hair cascaded over her shoulders. A black, spiky crown gleamed on her head.

On either side of her stood rows of fae draped in silver cloth. They wore crowns of rowan leaves with red berries. Presumably, they were the High Council, and their grumpy expressions told me they were not pleased to have been roused out of bed in the middle of the night.

Queen Brigantia—Ruadan's sister—looked oddly relaxed, considering a reported traitor and possible rival for the throne had just burst in here with an iron sword and two random, half-naked fae.

"Of all the things I could have imagined when my servant woke me at three in the morning, the last thing I would have expected was the sight of my brother arriving, dripping wet, with a barely clothed demi-fae and a small-footed prince from another land."

I was amazed that she recognized Maddan, but maybe all the fae royals knew each other.

The queen leaned forward. "What is this about you being a traitor? I'd only just received word from Grand Master Savus that you'd betrayed the Institute. He wanted permission to execute you. I said no, of course."

Ruadan straightened, his shadows darkening the air around him. He nodded at me. "Arianna is my novice. Prince Maddan is a traitor to the Institute and to Emain. I've brought him here to testify. Grand Master Savus has been compromised. He is working with Baleros, who is demanding my execution in exchange for the World Key.

Baleros wants to open the worlds again, to unleash chaos and recreate his gladiatorial arenas."

The queen narrowed her violet eyes—the same shade as Ruadan's. "Why would Savus work with Baleros? Baleros slaughtered our mother."

"Baleros has figured out exactly how to control Savus," said Ruadan. "He claims that he has a very important hostage."

The queen's eyes widened. "Who?"

Ruadan spoke again in Ancient Fae, his voice booming off the walls. I had no idea what he was saying until he switched back to English. "Our mother."

The Fae High Council began murmuring to one another, while Queen Brigantia's eyes were locked entirely on her brother. She didn't move, her body taking on that strange, animal stillness Ruadan so often displayed.

A ghostly wind whipped through the hall, and the queen's pale hair danced around her head. "You found our mother's body in her bedchamber."

Ruadan's body was as still as his sister's. "She'd been burned beyond recognition. It may have been another victim. Alternately, Baleros may be lying. But the important part is that Grand Master Savus believes Baleros, and he is now essentially an agent working for the traitor."

One of the High Council members stepped forward, her white hair piled high on her head. "You have a witness?"

Ruadan shoved Maddan forward. "He has been working with both Baleros and Grand Master Savus. Before I opened the portal, he was about to drive an iron sword through my throat. Arianna's as well."

The line of sentinels closed in around Maddan, swords pointed at him. Maddan's limbs were visibly shaking. "I was only acting as the Grand Master instructed," he protested. "He told me the Old Gods supported it, that once I did their bidding, I'd become one of the Shadow Fae."

The queen tapped her fingernails on the rocky throne. "There was a time when we were reluctant to torture royalty from other lands. It caused certain diplomatic problems, like wars. Invasions. But now, the worlds are locked. My brother is one of the few people with the power to open and close the portals. Your family cannot come for us. I'm afraid we must know the truth."

"It's all true!" Maddan shouted. "It's all true. Baleros has been sending Queen Macha's fingers to Grand Master Savus. Savus loves her. He only wanted to save her life."

The queen leaned back in her chair. "Torture him to make sure he's telling the truth."

Her logic made no sense whatsoever, and yet I was happy to jump in. I raised my hand. "Can I help with that?"

The queen nodded once.

I took a step closer to Maddan, and slammed my fist into his jaw. He tried blocking my blows with his forearms, but I dodged around them. I hit him in the ribs, the skull, cracking his nose. The sting on my knuckles felt glorious.

Then, I took a step back. Blood streamed from Maddan's nose.

The queen looked at him again, expectantly. "Well?"

Blood dripped down his hands. "Yes. It's exactly what I said before. Grand Master Savus was trying to save your mother by complying with Baleros's demands. He wants to steal the World Key from Ruadan's body."

The queen straightened. "So the leader of the Institute is no longer serving the Shadow Fae. Instead, he serves a traitor."

The High Council began arguing with one another, voices echoing off the ceiling. But they were speaking in Ancient Fae, and I had no idea what they were saying. After a minute, they seemed to come to some sort of a consensus, nodding and stepping back into their line.

The queen cocked her head. "Imprison the fae prince in the Institute. Assassinate Grand Master Savus. Assume control of London. Then, find Baleros. We will send word to the Shadow Fae institutes across the world. Report back to me, and do not waste any more time."

The sentinels closed in around Maddan, binding his arms behind his back. They clamped iron around his wrists.

The queen rose from her throne. "Aithmóre."

Ruadan repeated the fae word. Whatever it meant, the sound of it rumbled over my skin.

The sentinels stepped away, and Ruadan's body began to glow, his magic pulsing and rippling over my skin. As I felt the floor rumbling again, I prepared myself. When the first cracks appeared in the marble, I reached for the iron sword I'd dropped.

Churning waters appeared through the fissures, and the floor fell out from underneath us. I plunged into the icy water. The portal's watery depths enveloped me once more.

We had what we wanted—a directive to kill the Grand Master. But as I sank deeper into the portal, I had to wonder if Baleros was already one step ahead of us. It seemed he always was.

CHAPTER 33

Warm light glimmered on the portal's watery surface, and I kicked my legs. I wasn't entirely sure where the portal would be opening until I reached the air. Gasping, I scrambled for the stony ledge. The smell of mildew, must, and an undercurrent of blood hit me like a wave.

Ruadan brought us to one of the empty torture rooms in the dungeons, which was smart. It was completely empty down here.

Given the mist army situation, the only way to kill Grand Master Savus would be through a stealth assassination—not exploding into the Tower Green in a hail of water and rock. Another benefit was the arsenal of weapons glinting from one of the rocky walls.

I climbed over the ledge, and Ruadan turned back to the portal. When Maddan's ginger hair breached the surface, Ruadan hauled his shackled body out of the water.

Lying on his side, Maddan coughed up water onto the stone.

Ruadan gripped him by the shoulders and began dragging

him off to a cell in the other direction. Maddan's tiny bare feet left trails of water on the stone behind him.

My muscles tensed. I couldn't quite explain it, but something felt wrong in the air. The hair on my arms stood on end. Icy water dripped off my body, and I gripped the hilt of the sword, prowling slowly down the corridor, away from Ruadan.

I heard the sound of a cell door creaking, then slamming shut as Ruadan locked Maddan inside. The prince of Elfame was screaming something, his voice rattling with rage, but I blocked him out, trying to attune my senses to the Institute.

Faintly, Ruadan's footsteps sounded behind me, and I turned to him. "Something isn't right."

Ruadan gripped a broadsword that he'd pulled off the wall. "What do you sense?"

I bit my lip. I couldn't explain my sense of unease. "I don't know. Just—we need to be cautious."

His gaze flicked to the lumen stone at my neck. "Okay, but time is of the essence. The longer we spend here, the greater the chance we'll be discovered before we assassinate the Grand Master. Once we get to the Tower Green, I'm going to shadow-leap to Savus's chamber. I'll slaughter him within seconds. It will all be over."

I had complete faith in Ruadan's killing abilities, and yet as we climbed the dank stairwell, I couldn't shake the feeling that something was very wrong here at the Institute.

By the time we reached the top of the stairs, my chest was pounding.

Then, just before Ruadan pushed through the door to the Tower Green, it hit me like a fist to the gut.

The scent of roses.

Baleros's scent.

I gripped Ruadan's arm, pulling him back. On my tiptoes, I whispered into his ear, "He's here. Baleros is here."

Grand Master Savus had failed in his task of slaughtering Ruadan. Maybe Baleros thought he had to do the job himself.

Baleros's nineteenth law of power: Never send a servant to do the work of a king.

When Ruadan met my gaze, his eyes were as black as the void, and a chill slid through my bones. As we stood behind the oak door, mist curled under it, twining around us.

I frowned at the magical fog. Was Grand Master Savus deploying his mist army, or...

I gripped Ruadan's arm tighter, sliding the puzzle pieces together in my mind. "Do you really think Baleros would stick around here, facing the Grand Master's mist army in person? My old master doesn't face opponents he can't beat." My heart slammed against my ribs. "If Baleros is already here—"

My breath caught in my lungs, and I pulled open the door just a little, peering outside. My stomach sank at what I saw.

My old master—Baleros—prowled across the flowery green, a lumen stone glowing around his neck. The mist army surrounded him, fog lifting off of them in steamy tufts.

Panic climbed up my spine, and I closed the door again. As I did, another deep bell began to toll—just like the one in Emain.

"There's good news, and there's bad news," I whispered. "The good news, is we don't have to worry about killing Grand Master Savus. He's already dead. The bad news is that Baleros is now ten times more powerful than he was before, because he can shadow-leap and he's assumed control of the mist—"

A loud boom and the splintering of wood cut off the rest of my sentence. A battle-ax splintered the door, and mist began pooling inside.

"He controls the mist army," I said, completing my thought.

"Use the lumen stone," said Ruadan.

He didn't have to tell me twice. Without it, Baleros would corner us here in the dungeons. His mist army would slaughter us.

Through the shattering door, I glimpsed the darkened towers. I let my mind meld with the shadows across the green, and dark magic whispered through my blood.

I shadow-leapt outside, the wind whipping at my damp, half-naked body. I landed hard in a dark spot by a tower archway. Then, I whirled to find a small cohort of mist soldiers closing in on me. Just beyond them, I glimpsed Shadow Fae knights running out of the towers, swords raised. They were responding to the alarm, attacking the invaders.

Already, I'd lost track of Baleros, but I had a more pressing concern in the form of the ten mist soldiers closing in on me.

Shadow magic skimmed and buzzed over my skin, and I mentally bonded with the shadows behind them. I used the lumen stone to leap out of the circle of mist warriors. From behind them, I swung my sword into their backs. But instead of hitting flesh, it was like swiping through steam. How were we supposed to kill these guys?

My gaze flicked to Ruadan, who moved so fast I could barely track him. I saw only puffs of steam as my mentor carved his sword through the mist soldiers. Too bad the attacks didn't kill them. They simply wafted away like smoke, then solidified elsewhere in the green.

I shadow-leapt away from the mist soldiers, sniffing the air until I tuned into the scent of roses. The sickly-sweet scent dripped over the whole Institute. I could smell Baleros, but I couldn't see him.

Two mist soldiers ran for me. I whirled and leapt, my sword clashing against the mist soldiers' blades. Adrenaline blazed through my limbs as steel met steel. Still, every time I thrust my blade at them, it met only air. The fruitless attacks were throwing me off balance.

Everything could be killed. But how?

As I fought them, I kept scanning the Tower Green, searching for Baleros. I glimpsed the other Shadow Fae fighting the mist soldiers, but Baleros had hidden himself somewhere, letting his army do the work for him.

His absence was making me nervous. As usual, he was much more in control of this situation than Ruadan and I were. He knew where we were—and we had no idea where he'd gone.

I lunged into another mist soldier, my blade slicing steam. I'd worked up a sweat now, and I'd killed not a single soldier.

As cold sweat dripped down my gossamer gown, a fiery glow appeared through one of the Institute's arches. Baleros had committed his soul to the fire goddess. My heart thrummed. Was that him?

I had no doubt it was—my old master, about to unleash fiery hell on the Tower.

I summoned my shadow magic from the lumen stone, a cold burst of power. Then, I shadow-leapt closer to the archway. When I landed, I staggered back.

Baleros crossed through the archway, dragging someone with him. He was holding a knife to Ciara's throat. Of course the fucker had leverage.

His body glowed with orange light, and he was chanting a spell in the Angelic language. As he did, the sky blazed with searing light, fires in the heavens. It took me a moment to realize what he was doing.

With the fiery light he'd created in the sky above us, Baleros had burned out all the shadows. He'd made it impossible to shadow-leap anywhere.

My mind was a wild animal, ready to tear down everything in my path, but I had to move carefully, or Ciara would die. I froze, staring at Baleros, waiting to see what he'd demand of me. Drop my sword? Go with him? I'd do whatever he wanted to get Ciara away from him.

"What do you want from me?" I said through gritted teeth. "You have your leverage. What do you want?"

His lip curled. "Only to watch you suffer. You defied me. People need to learn there is a price for defiance."

Rage coursed through my body, and I went completely still.

Guilt gripped my heart. If it hadn't been for me, Ciara would never have been pulled into any of this. Baleros never would have brought her into the arena as my servant. He would never have brought her here.

My senses had become heightened. I felt the slither of mist over my skin, the distant heat of Baleros's glow. I felt the rush of Ruadan's shadow magic as he leapt over to us. I sensed the chilly, damp air of the mist soldiers closing in on us, their swords drawn.

I lifted my hand, signaling to Ruadan that he needed to be still. One false move, and Ciara was dead.

And yet my mind couldn't work out what to do next.

This wasn't leverage anymore. This was punishment.

Baleros was going to kill Ciara before my eyes.

"Watch your friend as she burns," said Baleros, and icy dread crashed into me.

For the briefest of moments, Baleros released Ciara, and she ran for me under the blazing light of the sky. Then, he hurled an enormous fireball at her body.

I stared, my mind reeling as she ignited, and her clothing and skin caught fire.

I started to run for her, desperate to stamp out the flames.

It took me a moment to realize she wasn't screaming, or writhing. Instead, she was simply transforming.

Great tendrils of red hair snaked around her head like flames. Her back arched, and her skin became ashy and cracked, with lava flowing beneath the fissured surface. But within the fire, she was *smiling*, her features ecstatic.

Behind her, Baleros's face looked as shocked as I felt. He hadn't seen this coming, either.

She grinned at me. "The devil wears many faces," she hissed.

I stared as the clothing burned off her body.

I hardly registered the darkness falling around us, the light receding from the sky.

Then, Ciara eyed me through the fires that licked around her body.

What in the hells...?

She took another step closer to me. "Arianna. Behind you."

I blinked, completely at a loss for words. When I felt a cold lick of steam at my neck, I whirled again to slash my sword. A mist soldier puffed into the air. To my right, Ruadan was trying to fend off another group of mist soldiers, his sword clanging.

I turned back to Ciara, my legs shaking. "What the fuck, Ciara? You look like a gods-damn demon. You *are* a gods-damn demon."

She pointed again. "Behind you."

I spun. A sharp arc of my blade slammed into a mist soldier, vaporizing him.

She looked down at her own blazing hands, fire curling from her skin. "I always thought the McDougall family legends were true." Then, she met my gaze, fire burning in her pupils. "Didn't I tell you I'd protect you if it came down to it? I told you my grandma was from the embers under a mountain, didn't I? I sensed something bad was about to happen. I could feel it behind my knees, like when a storm is coming. Baleros captured me, but I wasn't scared. A McDougall woman always gets out alive."

My jaw dropped open. *Things really aren't always what they seem.* "I thought you were human. What the hells are you?"

"I've been telling you and telling you. The devil wears many faces." Flames erupted from her eyes, and a long tongue of fire unfurled from her mouth.

I ducked, narrowly missing the flames.

Without another word, she leapt into the center of the mist army. Swaths of flames curled off her body, snaking around the soldiers. As the fiery magic touched their bodies, they hissed, evaporating like steam. The air felt heavy with water as Ciara's fire singed the mist soldiers. I stared at the steam curling up into the heavens. She was actually destroying them, when our blades couldn't.

Ciara really *was* protecting me, this creature forged in the fiery depths of a mountain. And all this time, I'd thought she was the one who needed me.

I didn't have much time to gape at this transformation. A battle still raged here at the Institute, while Baleros was fighting to slaughter the Wraith. Speaking of the Wraith, where had he gone?

While I'd been staring at Ciara, Baleros and Ruadan had both leapt away once more.

My old master's rosewater scent coiled through the air like a miasma, a smell that would forever make me sick. I desperately needed to end him, to rid my skull of his phantom presence. As long as he lived, Baleros would always be one step ahead of me, living in my mind, predicting my moves before I made them.

And worse, if he lived, Baleros would tell everyone the truth about me.

Frantically, I searched the green for Ruadan, for Baleros. And when I saw them, my heart stopped.

With dozens of mist soldiers surrounding him, Ruadan didn't see Baleros shadow-leaping behind him. He didn't notice that Baleros was raising an iron sword.

I didn't think. I just leapt, fury erupting like a volcano. I needed Baleros's blood on my hands. I landed just behind Baleros with a hard thud. As he whirled, I thrust my iron blade into his heart, thrilled at the feel of my blade carving into his chest.

It took me a moment to feel the pain fracturing my own body…just a moment to realize that while I'd been stabbing Baleros, he'd thrust his sword into me at the same time.

The blood drained from my skull as I stared down at Baleros's iron sword protruding from my heart.

The world started to dim, and I heard Ruadan shouting my name as if from a great distance. His magic rippled over me, trying to pull me back from death.

Before I died, I had just enough time for a single thought to pass through my mind.

I always knew I'd die at the hand of Baleros.

CHAPTER 34

Darkness enveloped me, and I felt myself falling through space. Weightless, unmoored.

I plummeted for hours, tumbling through a void.

I'd always thought death would be peaceful, a long sleep. This was not peaceful. No, it was pure panic, endless regret, and sorrow that cut me to the marrow. I longed to feel the light on my skin again, to hear the sounds of birds calling, to skim my fingers over a lake's surface. I needed to wrap my arms around Ruadan, around Ciara. I needed answers from them, needed their stories completed in my mind. I yearned to breathe in the scent of Ruadan's neck as I lay under the blankets with him, limbs entangled.

Emptiness cut me to the bone.

I fell faster, wind tearing at my hair. When I'd been alive, this darkness, this death, had dwelled inside me like a cancer. I'd filled the void with chatter, with whiskey and blood. And I wanted those things now more than ever. And more. More. A wild hunger tore through me. I wanted to feel Ruadan's skin against mine, to skim my teeth over his neck, to run through a forest with brambles scratching my legs, and to swim through clear, cold waters.

I plunged ever downward—until a powerful set of arms caught me. I gasped, endlessly relieved to feel the solidity of another body.

Pale blue eyes blazed over me, flecked with gold. I'd know those eyes anywhere. Eyes that haunted my nightmares. *Death.*

He leaned down, breathing into my mouth, and warmth blossomed in my lungs.

* * *

I OPENED MY EYES, gasping. Pain racked my body, and I gripped my heart. A wound gaped in my chest. And yet…

I was alive. I'd come back to life.

If I could come back to life, that meant…

It took me a moment to realize someone was cradling me, and I looked up into Ruadan's black eyes. For a second, I took in the pain etched on his features. Then, the shock as he realized my eyes had opened.

I clutched my chest, gasping. Pain still coursed through my muscles, until Ruadan's magic slid over my skin. It soothed the hurt.

"How are you alive?" he asked, his voice rough and jagged.

I held my hand over the gaping wound in my chest, and I simply shook my head. I'd thought of him in death. Who could have imagined that my dying thoughts would turn to the Wraith? Things were definitely not always as they seemed.

"Never mind," said Ruadan. "Don't try to speak. You killed Baleros." The scent of burnt flesh filled the air, and smoke curled behind Ruadan's head. "The fire goddess will bring him back." Ruadan's pale hair caught in the wind, and he cocked his head, studying me closely with those black eyes. "He killed you. He drove an iron sword into your heart. You were dead."

I loosed a long breath. *Death is difficult to kill.*

He leaned down, and his breath warmed the shell of my ear. "What are you?"

A nightmare. I said nothing. I'd learned from the best.

His magic still whispered over my body, leaching away the pain. I wanted sleep more than anything. I rested my head against his powerful chest, and I closed my eyes.

* * *

I SAT before a mirror while Ciara did her best to smooth my hair over the back of my long gown. Silver chinks shimmered on the sheer fabric like stars, and its violet hue matched the lumen stone around my neck.

My oldest friend's skin looked normal again, but fire still licked in her eyes. Apparently, this was the new Ciara.

Moonlight streamed in through the windows. I had my own room now—one covered in wildflowers, with a bath of my own.

It had only been three days day since Baleros had rammed an iron blade into my heart, and a deep scar still marred my chest. Ruadan's magic hadn't been able to fully heal the skin, but he'd mended everything inside me, knitting together arteries and muscles with his magic. Now, I felt only a dull ache in the center of my chest.

Ciara took a hairbrush to my hair, and I winced at the sharp tug of the bristles through my tangles.

I glanced at Ciara, whose red hair still snaked around her head.

"You never told me you were a demon," I said.

She shrugged. "I didn't know. Just kind of came out. I told you my grandma came from a volcano, didn't I?"

My lips twitched in a smile. "We'll make a formidable gods-damn team, you know that?"

"Ciarianna has risen again." She yanked at my hair, tugging my snarls into submission with the brutal hairbrush. "And now, you're about to be knighted as a Shadow Fae by Grand Master Ruadan. Are you ready for it?"

I stared at myself in the mirror. For just a moment, darkness flitted through my eyes, and weightlessness tugged at my chest. Then, my mind cleared. "I'm ready. Now, you'd better get the hells out of here before someone finds you."

"They still don't want me here?"

"No, Ciara. We're supposed to slaughter demons. That hasn't changed."

She blew a strand of her hair out of her eyes with a sigh. "Fine. Good luck with your knighthood. I'm coming back to check on you." She jabbed me in the ribs. "And we need to fatten you up. You're too thin." Then she crossed to the center of the room. Fire blazed around her, a small tornado of flames that consumed her body. When the fire burned out, she left nothing behind but a few ashes and the scent of smoke.

I coughed. I'd need to think of some way to explain the scent of burned flesh that the New Ciara left behind whenever she departed.

A knock sounded at my door, and I crossed to it. I pulled it open and smiled at the sight of Melusine. She still wore a violet lumen stone around her neck.

"Melusine!" I beamed. "Did you return just for the knighting ceremony?"

She nodded. "That, and I live here now. I wanted to come

back, and I hear about this job opening and I think, *that's my chance*. Turns out, the librarian can't fly around so well anymore. Got a skull fracture in a Segway accident. So I show up and I say, you know what? I belong in the library, on account of my superior intellectual skills. I can read in over three languages. English, Ancient Fae, Modern Fae, and English written by Scottish people."

"Nice."

"Yeah, I'm pretty good at stuff."

I smoothed my hair over my shoulder. I felt oddly nervous for this ceremony, unaccustomed to this sort of attention. "Want to walk with me to the knighting?"

"Yeah, let's go." And without another word, she began stomping down the hallway.

I hurried to catch up with her.

As she crossed into the stairwell, she shot me a puzzled look. "Hey, why did it smell like smoke in your room?"

I cleared my throat. "I've been smoking."

She shook her head. "No, it did not smell like tobacco. It smelled like burnt flesh."

I traced my fingers over the stone walls as we descended, and I tried to think of a plausible lie. "I roasted a squirrel."

Nope. Nope. Not a good one.

"I heard a fire demon took out part of the mist army," she said, as we reached the bottom of the stairwell. "A friend of yours. Not supposed to be in this realm anymore though, is she? I put two and two together." Before pushing through the door, she stared at me for a long time. At last, she said, "Not my problem. I'm just the librarian."

She stepped out onto the night-dark Tower Green. Shadow magic pulsed around her body, and she leapt across the green to the white stone Cailleach Tower.

For a moment, my eyes flicked across the Green to the

spot where Baleros had driven a blade through my heart. My breath caught in my lungs. That feeling of weightlessness whispered through my blood, dizzying me.

I faltered, then focused again on the feel of my feet on the stony earth, rooting me in place. I was here, my feet solidly on the ground. I was alive. *Breathe in. Breathe out.*

Then, I shadow-leapt to the entrance of the Cailleach Tower. The oak door stood open, and I crossed inside.

The silk gown brushed against my legs as I walked. I wasn't used to wearing such delicate fabrics, but I liked the way the dress draped over my body. Even better, I liked imagining what the new Grand Master's face would look like when he saw me in it.

I smiled to myself as I crossed into the Great Hall.

The last time I'd been in here, I'd been standing over an execution block, while Maddan smirked at me, awaiting my demise.

Aengus, Melusine, and the others lined either side of the hall, waiting to see me knighted.

Ruadan sat in the rocky throne on the dais, and a silver crown gleamed on his head.

Baleros might have the mist army, but Ruadan had the crown and the blessing of Emain. Now Ruadan ruled London's Institute of the Shadow Fae.

And just as I'd imagined, his eyes bored right into me, drinking in the sight of the thin, silky gown. A smile curled my lips. He might be the ruler here, but I had my own sort of power over him, and I wanted to see how far I could push that.

I'd never wanted to be a spell-slayer, never imagined myself as an enforcer of arbitrary laws. But now, as I walked deeper into the hall before Ruadan, a thrill washed over me.

Now I belonged somewhere.

Ruadan rose as I crossed to him, and he drew his sword. Just before the dais, I knelt on the stone floor. This time, I didn't mind kneeling.

Ruadan stood over me, speaking in Ancient Fae. I couldn't understand what he was saying, but as he spoke, starry magic whirled around me. For just a moment, I felt myself falling again, but I focused on the feel of my knees and shins on the stone floor.

As Ruadan tapped the sword on my shoulder, a crackling power imbued my muscles. At last, he commanded me to rise. I stood, looking into his violet eyes. I'm pretty sure I saw pride glinting there.

Then, he leaned down, whispering into my ear, "What are you, Arianna?"

I smiled at him, then turned to walk away.

Let's see how well The Wraith liked the silent treatment.

THANK you for reading Court of Shadows. This book is part of the *Demons of Fire and Night* world. Caine and Bael appear in the *Vampires's Mage* and *Shadows and Flame* series, and the *Spy Among the Fallen* series is also part of the same world.

If you want to grab a set of free stories in the Demons of Fire and Night World, click here.

Join us on Facebook!

ALSO BY C.N. CRAWFORD

For a full list of our books, check out our website.

https://www.cncrawford.com/books/

And a possible reading order.

https://www.cncrawford.com/faq/

ACKNOWLEDGMENTS

Thanks to my supportive family, and to Michael Omer for his fantastic feedback and help managing my many author crises. Thanks to Nick for his insight and help crafting the book.

Robin Marcus and Blair Schuyler are my fabulous editors. Thanks to my advanced reader team for their help, and to C.N. Crawford's Coven on Facebook!

Made in the USA
Middletown, DE
17 September 2023

38670817R00144